"You dare say th
who deprived o
her father for t

His night-black eyes leaping with violence bored into hers as he continued. "Deprived me of my child." He focused on her with a dark blistering anger that heightened the tension to breaking point. "I saw you today on the beach and I wanted to kill you. Three years of hell you put me through. I am going to make sure you suffer as I have," he hissed with lethal intent.

The fear and tension that had held her since the moment he had walked back into her life finally snapped and Kelly exploded. "Make me suffer! You did that from the day you married me. You never wanted me. All you ever wanted was my child...."

JACQUELINE BAIRD began writing as a hobby when her family objected to the smell of her oil painting, and immediately became hooked on the romance genre. She loves traveling and worked her way around the world from Europe to the Americas and Australia, returning to marry her teenage sweetheart. She lives in Northumbria, UK, where she was born, and has two teenage sons. She enjoys playing badminton, and spends most weekends with husband Jim, sailing their Gp. 14 around Derwent Reservoir.

Books by Jacqueline Baird

HARLEQUIN PRESENTS®
2088—HUSBAND ON TRUST
2137—A MOST PASSIONATE REVENGE
2196—MARRIAGE AT HIS CONVENIENCE

Jacqueline Baird

THE ITALIAN'S RUNAWAY BRIDE

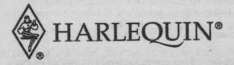

HARLEQUIN®

TORONTO • NEW YORK • LONDON
AMSTERDAM • PARIS • SYDNEY • HAMBURG
STOCKHOLM • ATHENS • TOKYO • MILAN • MADRID
PRAGUE • WARSAW • BUDAPEST • AUCKLAND

ISBN 0-373-12219-5

THE ITALIAN'S RUNAWAY BRIDE

First North American Publication 2001.

Copyright © 2001 by Jacqueline Baird.

CHAPTER ONE

KELLY MCKENZIE, skimpily clad in cut-off denim shorts and shirt, lay flat on her back on the lawn that sloped softly to the edge of Lake Garda, and sighed her contentment. It was the end of August; the sun was shining and life was great. Rolling onto her stomach, she looked back at the house, a glorious old stone building set some fifty yards from the water's edge. A terrace extended across the full width of the house, and at one end a cluster of cypress trees and shrubs cascaded over the stone balustrades. Shrubs that appeared to be moving, although there was not a breath of wind! How odd!

Then she saw him. Her blue eyes narrowed warily. It was the figure of a man half-hidden by the bushes; one hand was on the balustrade and he was leaning over, trying to peer into a window. In his other hand was an iron bar. Kelly's heart missed a beat. Suspicious didn't cover it... He looked downright dangerous.

Every muscle of her body filled with tension. She watched as he straightened up, his back to her. Dressed in a white vest and a pair of oil-stained khaki shorts, he looked thoroughly disreputable. He was tall—well over six feet—broad-shouldered with lean hips, and he had long legs that rippled with muscle and sinew as he moved.

A man who was moving furtively towards the steps up to the terrace and the entrance to the rear windows of the house...

Stay cool, girl, she told herself, you can handle this. Three months ago, when she'd bumped into an old school

5

friend, Judy Bertoni, in Bournemouth, and Judy had offered her a job as a nanny to her son with the family in Italy for ten weeks, Kelly had leapt at the chance to spend a summer in the sun, before taking up her post as a research chemist with a government laboratory in Dorset in October.

It had seemed a great idea at the time, but now, faced with what looked like a very sinister intruder, Kelly was not so sure...

She was on her own. The family was in Rome, and Marta the housekeeper had taken the opportunity of her employer's absence to go and visit friends, after having warned Kelly to lock up carefully as there had been a spate of burglaries in the area.

Kelly fought down the panicked urge to leap up and run and sat silently watching the figure of the man move stealthily to the first step. The tyre iron in his hand said it all. He was obviously intent on breaking in.

Well, there was nothing for it, Kelly told herself: desperate situations required desperate remedies, and she'd been a keen gymnast in her youth and the university Thai kick-boxing champion two years running. While the intruder's attention was firmly fixed on the windows of the house she psyched herself into fighting mode. Slowly, silently she rose to her feet, adrenaline pumping through her veins.

Then, with a blood-curdling yell, she spun through the air like a whirlwind, and in a few deft kicks the would-be burglar was flat on his back and she had the tyre iron in her hand and her foot on his throat.

Gianfranco Maldini had spun around in surprise at the noise, then he'd had a fleeting image of silver-blonde hair and a very feminine form flying towards him, then all the air had left his lungs.

He could not believe it... A chit of a girl had quite literally dumped him flat on his back. Never in all of his thirty-one years had a woman done that to *him*. About to move, he glanced up the long shapely length of her and stilled. His testosterone took over from common sense.

Dio, but she was gorgeous. His dark eyes raked over her in a slow, intense scrutiny. From the top of her head, where silver-blonde hair had been scraped back into a pony-tail and tied with a ribbon, lingering on the perfect symmetry of her features, wild eyes, and a sultry mouth that was begging to be kissed, then lower, to where her high firm breasts pushed against the soft cotton shirt she had knotted under the luscious mounds. An expanse of smooth pale flesh revealed her tiny waist and the indentation of her navel, which the ridiculously ragged denim shorts could not hide, nor the long shapely legs.

For the first time in years Gianfranco was struck dumb; he felt himself instantly harden and that had not happened in years either, he thought wryly. But she was stunningly beautiful, vibrant with life, and the image of her flying through the air with such verve and grace was the most spectacular thing he had seen in a long time. What she was doing at Carlo Bertoni's he had no idea, but it might be a lot of fun to find out. He had not had a holiday in three years and uncomplicated fun had been sadly lacking in his life of late, he suddenly realised. A quick call to his office, and he could free up some time. New York could wait. Yes, he was going to pursue her, he decided with unconscious arrogance.

He could do without her foot on his neck, but he was in no hurry to get up. The view was stunning. She was standing legs apart, one leg bent at the knee to keep her foot on his throat and the other beside his shoulder. Her shorts did not cover all they should and he made the intriguing discovery that she was a natural blonde and he had to smile as he wondered if she knew what she was exposing.

Kelly lifted the tyre iron in her hand, finally getting a good look at the burglar. Thick black hair flopped over his broad forehead in soft curls and perfectly arched black eyebrows framed deep brown heavily lidded eyes. Only a slight crook in what once must have been a straight blade of a nose stopped him from being classically beautiful. But the whole added up to a ruggedly handsome man. A wickedly handsome man, she amended when his lips curved back over brilliant white teeth in a slow, sexy smile.

Kelly almost groaned out loud. Why was it that the most gorgeous male she had seen in her life was a thief? Even at her mercy, he had an aura of supreme male confidence about him that was hard to ignore. But that did not make him any less a burglar, she told herself staunchly. More likely it meant he was highly successful at his chosen occupation.

'Now, look here, buster, I know you came here to commit a burglary.'

'What?' Gianfranco exclaimed. Being caught off-guard and thrown to the ground was humiliating enough, but to be accused of being a thief was a step too far for a man of his pride and arrogance. In that second he vowed he would make the little madam pay for the insult.

'Don't play the innocent with me—it won't wash,' Kelly blundered on determinedly. 'But I am prepared to give you a chance. You didn't actually get around to stealing anything, so I will let you go, if you promise not to come back.'

The man on the ground shook his head in amazement. If the girl really thought he was a criminal, she was hopelessly naïve believing a genuine thief would just walk away.

'Was that a no?' Kelly demanded, seeing him shake his head. 'Because the alternative is I am going to hit you over the head with this iron bar, and call the police.'

'No—yes,' Gianfranco spluttered, his sense of humour totally deserting him as he noticed she was holding the damned tyre iron over her head. She was mad, and he had wasted too long lying on the ground admiring the view.

One minute Kelly was congratulating herself on keeping her head and control of the man and situation, the next, with a speed that defied gravity, their positions were reversed. Her head hit the ground with a thump and for a second she saw stars, and when her vision cleared she was pinned to the ground. Her hands were held above her head in one massive male hand, and a great body was splayed half over her, one long muscular leg flung across her own slender limbs.

'Get off me! You great brute!' she yelled, and started to struggle, but to very little effect. He was much bigger and much stronger. He simply tightened his hold on her wrists and with his free hand he caught her chin, holding her head firm as he stared down at her with angry brown eyes.

'Now, why would I do that?' Gianfranco asked mockingly. 'If I am the villain you imagine, do you really think I am going to let you go?'

Kelly wasn't thinking, she was panicking, the iron bar she'd taken off him had vanished, and his chest felt like iron pressing down on hers. In a last desperate attempt to dislodge him she tried bringing her knee up against his thigh, and opened her mouth to scream.

She almost succeeded, but a hard mouth crashed down on hers and choked off the scream in her throat. It was a kiss of sheer power, forcing her lips back against her teeth until she thought he would draw blood. If he'd wanted to frighten her he had succeeded, she thought numbly.

Then subtly the kiss changed. His mouth gentled on hers, moving over and over against the lush fullness of her lips, and, to her shame, slowly she felt herself succumbing to the intense sensual pleasure his kiss aroused. Involuntarily her lips parted on a soft, needy sigh, and helplessly she accepted the probing invasion of his tongue.

His hand dropped from her chin to curve around the fullness of her breast, and time stopped. Heat flared through every vein in her body. Seduced by the touch of his hand, the heat of his kiss, the musky male scent of him, she melted against him. It had never happened to her before, sexual excitement overwhelming her mind and body.

When he finally broke the kiss and lifted his head she stared up at him in hazy puzzlement, wondering why he had stopped. His hand fell from her breast and he stared down at her with eyes black with anger. She felt the hard proof of his arousal against her belly, and suddenly she came to her senses. What was she inviting by her helpless surrender to his kiss?

Gianfranco, with the part of his brain that still functioned, wondered what the hell he was doing, making love to a crazy English girl on the lawn of his friends' house in the middle of the day. Even though another much more basic part of him had responded instantly to the feel of her curvaceous body softening against him, it angered him. He was not the sort of man who ever lost control.

'Please let me go,' Kelly pleaded. Somehow he had inserted one long leg between her own and the heat and weight of him was no longer exciting but sexually threatening. This was a total stranger and a thief she was dealing with, and maybe worse, judging from the state of his body. 'Stop now,' she cried, fighting to stay calm. 'You know, you could go to prison for years for rape.'

'*Santa Maria.*' Incredulous dark eyes stared down into

the beautiful face of the woman beneath him. He had been accused of many things in his time, but a rapist certainly was not one of them. 'Are you completely mad?' he rasped scathingly.

'No.' The fact that his kiss had knocked her for a loop must have been an apparition, Kelly told herself. She knew what she had to do. He was angry and dangerous, she had to humour him until she got a chance to run.

'Who the hell are you? And what are you doing here?' Gianfranco demanded bluntly. Apart from driving him crazy, he thought wryly. He was very conscious of the soft subtle body...except it wasn't soft, but stiff with tension. He looked into the bluest eyes he had ever seen in his life, and saw she really was frightened, but doing her best to hide it. She actually believed the rubbish she'd been spouting.

'My name is Kelly McKenzie, and I am working here for the summer as a nanny to the owners' child.' If she could keep him talking, she had a better chance to escape. 'No one heard me scream, so if you let me go now I promise I will not report you.'

'*Basta.* Enough.' This farce had gone on long enough. Report him, indeed! Gianfranco saw her flinch, and determinedly forced himself to lower his tone. 'Well, Kelly McKenzie, I am not going to hurt you; I have never forced a woman in my life and I am not going to start with you. Understand?' She looked up into the dark attractive face, and wanted to believe him. 'Now, I am going to let go of you and we are going to sit up and discuss this mistake like two rational human beings. Agreed?'

She nodded, every muscle in her body tensing in anticipation of escape. The next moment he let go of her wrists and sat up, but before she could even move he had placed a strong arm around her slender shoulders and hauled her hard against him.

'Neither am I a burglar,' he continued quietly. 'So sit still and listen.'

She didn't have much option, with his hands linked in front of her, trapping her in the cage of his arms. But, with the imminent danger of rape fading from her mind, Kelly began to recover some of her usual feisty temperament.

'So you make a habit of wandering around other people's gardens with an iron bar?' She turned her head and arched one delicate eyebrow sardonically. Did the man take her for a complete idiot? she wondered. But to her surprise he started to chuckle, a deep, throaty sound that did uncomfortable things to her pulse rate again.

'Ah, Kelly, now I understand. I know Carlo Bertoni. I borrowed the tyre iron from him to fix a wheel on the boat trailer, down at the marina. I came around today to return it.'

She had never mentioned her employer's name and yet this man knew it, and she also knew Signor Bertoni kept a boat in the marina. Kelly almost groaned out loud. Such a simple explanation, but she had jumped to the worst possible scenario. Her own father had always used to tell her she had too much imagination for her own good. This time she had surpassed herself. The man spoke English but with an Italian accent. Obviously he must work at the harbour in Desenzano, and as he continued she felt the colour rise in her face.

'The security gate was open so I called at the door, and when no one answered I walked around the back with the intention of leaving the iron on the terrace. I didn't want to take it back with me, because I have another call to make further around the lake at Bardolino. That was until I saw this wild woman come flying at me like a circus tumbler and she immediately accused me of being a thief.'

'Oh, my God! I am sorry.' Kelly swivelled around, raising very relieved sparkling blue eyes to his. 'So you're not a thief but a sailor, and you work at the port in town.'

Gianfranco's lips quirked at the corners in the briefest of grins; he had never met a woman in his life before with the ability to jump to conclusions so readily. It crossed his mind to correct her but, looking down into her surprisingly guileless face, and lower to the soft thrust of her breasts, he remembered his earlier decision to have some fun. Plus, it still rankled she had floored him so easily.

'Yes, I do sail, and I have been working on a boat all morning.' He didn't lie, but neither was he telling the truth.

'I suppose this is the busiest time of year here on Lake Garda, what with all the tourists. Then, of course, there is the big race next week—the contestants come from all over the world, I understand.' Her employer was going to sail in the twenty-four-hour race. 'I suppose that is how you speak such good English.' Kelly was babbling, she knew, but she was so relieved he wasn't a criminal, just an ordinary person like herself. Now no longer afraid of him, she suddenly had a terrific urge to simply relax in the curve of his arm.

'Maybe,' he said with a smile, his dark brown eyes glittering as they met her trusting blue. 'But allow me to introduce myself. Gianfranco…'

'How do you do, Signor Franco?' Nerves and a racing pulse made her jerk out her hand, a tentative smile illuminating her lovely face. 'May I call you Gian?'

'Gianni. I prefer Gianni.' And, with her hand swallowed up in his, he dragged her to her feet. 'So, Kelly, no more misunderstandings. Friends…as you English say, shake on it.'

Very formally they shook hands, but she could see the dancing lights in his deep brown eyes and she chuckled. Then she laughed out loud; the strength of his handclasp, the slight calluses she could feel against her soft palm, obviously from manual labour, convinced her he was telling the truth. 'I can't believe I thought you were a robber,' she spluttered, and then the spluttering stopped as he drew her close into the long length of his body.

'A kiss to seal our friendship.' And his dark head swooped down, his mouth claiming hers in a long, tender kiss.

When he finally eased her away from him she was trembling, bemused; her dazed blue eyes sought his, and as she watched his heavy-lidded eyes narrowed, masking his expression, and just for a second she wondered if she had accepted his explanation a little too easily.

'I am afraid I have to leave in a minute, but, now we have established we are friends, will you have dinner with me tonight? Or will Signor Bertoni object?' Gianfranco asked lightly, tucking her hand under his arm and leading her slowly around the side of the house.

'I'd love to,' Kelly accepted with alacrity. 'I have the next week free, because Signor Bertoni and his wife and son Andrea have gone to visit his parents in Rome.' Her tongue was running away with her, she knew, but with his fingers linked with hers, and her arm pressed against his side, a tingling sensation sizzled through her whole body; she felt as if she had been plugged into an electric socket. The sudden sensual shock to her system was something completely outside her experience.

'How old are you?' Gianfranco interrupted her rambling explanation, glancing down at the beautiful but nervous girl at his side with some amusement. He was far too astute not to recognise that her feverish response to his kiss had shocked her more than it had shocked him. Even so, he hadn't felt such an instant powerful attraction to a woman in years. She obviously did not have vast experience of the male sex, and it would be his pleasure to expand her education. He slashed her a smile, and felt a brief twinge of guilt; she didn't look much more than a teenager.

'I'm twenty-one.' Kelly beamed up at him. 'Why, how old are you?'

'Thirty-one—probably too old for you.'

'Not at all,' Kelly denied quickly. 'Judy is twelve years younger than Signor Bertoni, and they are very happily married. In fact, she would do anything for him. That is why I am here on my own. Judy likes to impress her in-laws by looking after her son herself when she visits them.'

Kelly had no idea how much she was giving away by her announcement, but to the man at her side it was a warning. Kelly McKenzie was not the type for a brief fling. She clearly believed in marriage and happy-ever-after and he knew he was on dangerous ground. But, looking down at her animated features and her luscious body, Gianfranco squashed his doubts. He wanted her, and he was a man who always got what he wanted...

Eight o'clock in the evening and Kelly's first surprise was Gianni's arrival on a large roaring motorbike. They dined on baked lake trout, sitting on the terrace of a small *trattoria* in a tiny village high up in the mountains. Far below them, the dark waters of Lake Garda shimmered in the moonlight, a perfect setting for a romantic meal.

It was well after midnight when they took their leave and got back on the bike. Kelly wrapped her slender arms around him, clasping her hands together at his waist and clinging tightly to him as he expertly manoeuvred the motorbike along the winding road back to Desenzano.

Handing Gianni back the crash helmet he had insisted she wear, Kelly was suddenly deflated that the evening was almost over. She looked up at the house and then back to Gianni. Should she ask him in? But it wasn't her house, and she had only just met him. 'Thank you for a lovely evening,' she began formally, but Gianni solved her problem by placing the helmets on the seat of the bike and drawing her slowly into his arms.

'The pleasure was all mine,' he husked softly, 'and, if you will permit me, I have a few days' holiday and I would like to spend them showing you around the lake.'

'Yes, please,' she agreed breathlessly, completely bemused by the slumbering sensuality in his dark eyes, and when he bent his head and kissed her her fate was sealed. He was everything she had ever wanted, dreamed of, she realised, and nothing else mattered in the world but to be in his arms, where she just *knew* she belonged.

CHAPTER TWO

THE next four days they spent touring on the motorbike to some of the lesser-known beauty spots. Places that only the locals knew, according to Gianni.

Kelly was fascinated and thrilled in turn; they laughed and teased, and talked. She discovered he lived on the other side of Desenzano, with his mother; his father had been dead for some years. It made sense because Kelly knew that the other side of the marina was the old town, so obviously Gianni was a local, and it was quite usual for an Italian male to live at home until he married.

Every day that passed her passion for Gianni grew, until finally she admitted to herself she was in love for the first time in her life.

Kelly lay flat on her back on the blanket Gianni had provided for their picnic. It was a beautiful spot—a small grassy clearing on the edge of the lake. They'd had to ride the bike through the trees to find it. But Gianni had assured her they were not trespassing. Slipping off her shorts and shirt to reveal a tiny blue bikini, she'd run into the cool water of the lake with Gianni chasing her. She could still feel the imprint of his large nearly naked body against hers as he had wrapped two strong arms around her and his firm mouth had closed over hers to kiss her breathless.

She turned her head slightly. Gianni was lying beside her, one arm outstretched and the other loosely curved around the top of her head. She watched the slow rise and fall of his mighty bronzed chest with helpless fascination. They had eaten lunch, fresh bread, a whole roast chicken, and fruit and cheese. Now he looked as if he was asleep and she could admire him to her heart's content.

Her eyes wandered with awe over his sinfully sexy body—tanned, with a smattering of soft black body hair over his chest arrowing down beneath the wicked black trunks that cupped his sex and not much more. She was beginning to regret not asking him into the house that very first night, because the next day Marta had returned and so now she couldn't, and she ached for him with fervour she could barely control.

Restlessly she sat up. Judy had called this morning— they were coming back the next day, Saturday, and her freedom to meet Gianni would be seriously curtailed. Helplessly her eyes strayed back to the man at her side and she frowned.

'Why the frown?' Gianni queried lazily, lifting heavy-lidded eyes to hers.

She had thought he was asleep and, catching the dark gleam in his slumbrous eyes, she knew he had been aware of her watching him, and liked it. Her heart jumped, and her nipples tightened against the brief cotton covering in unwitting response.

Drawing her knees up to her chin, and wrapping her arms around them, hiding as much of her body as she could, she fixed her eyes on the lake and said, 'The family are coming back tomorrow.' She had no real reason to be afraid their relationship would end simply because her brief holiday was ending. But she was... 'This is the last day of my holiday, I suppose,' she said with a brief attempt at a smile.

'Then we must not waste it,' Gianni drawled huskily, and, reaching up, he caught her shoulders and tumbled her round and down on top of him, his mouth finding hers with unerring accuracy. 'Open your mouth,' he husked against her lips, but he did not need to ask as she was more than willing.

Gianni's strong hands swept down the length of her slender body, shaping her waist and hips, her thighs, and trailed back up, one to settle on her buttocks, the other to inch up over her breast. His fingers slipped beneath her bikini top, his thumb grazing over one pert nipple, and she gasped into his mouth as her breast hardened at his touch. She felt his great body's instant reaction, and instinctively she straddled him, wanting his masculine hardness at the most sensitive part of her. She squirmed on top of him, only two bits of cloth separating her from the possession she ached for.

'*Dio*, I want you,' Gianni rasped. 'I have to have you.' He swallowed a groan.

She was all fire and light in his arms; the provocative sexiness of her incredible body moving against him made him dizzy with a raw, primitive desire he could barely control. It was years since he had made love to a girl out in the open, and he knew he should not do it now. He was a well-known man, the lake was full of boats, perhaps even paparazzi, which was the last thing he needed. He'd never realised until the last few days how difficult it was for lesser mortals to find somewhere to take a woman to bed. He should stop this now. But as he felt her breast swell into his hand, the soft, slightly tentative stroke of her tongue on his throat, he was lost.

Gianni rolled her over onto her back and nudged her thighs apart to settle himself in the cradle of her hips, his hands seeking the halter-neck of her top. He wanted to feast on her beauty, to touch and taste every delectable inch of her. But first his mouth angled over her pouting lips in a kiss of wild, hungry passion. Then he heard it...

Suddenly Kelly found herself staring up into the bright sun glinting down from a clear blue sky. Gianni had leapt up, a string of what had sounded very like curses escaping from his mouth in a low, furious undertone.

She sat up. Gianni was striding to the edge of the trees, where a much older man stood with a shotgun over his arm. She couldn't hear what was said, and in any case she was too embarrassed. She hadn't heard the other man approach. Thank heaven Gianni had or the poor old fellow might have got the shock of his life.

Horribly embarrassed by what had nearly happened, she jerked to her feet. Never mind what Gianni had said, she just *knew* they must be trespassing, and they had been caught. Panic-stricken, she began bundling everything together, visions of languishing in an Italian jail leaping into her mind.

'I don't believe it,' Gianni muttered furiously under his breath, swinging around and striding back to pick up his shorts and shirt and pull them on.

'We are trespassing, aren't we?' Kelly demanded, her face flushed, her hair disheveled. She had no notion of how wonderful she looked to Gianni as she struggled into her own shorts and top.

A wry smile parted his firm mouth. He'd just been caught by the security guard he employed to keep an eye on the grounds and hunting lodge he owned. At least the man was doing his job properly, but it was no consolation to Gianni, who was aching in actual pain with frustration. Not for the first time in the last few days he wondered if the pretence was worth it. But he was so used to women throwing themselves at him because of his wealth and name that it made a refreshing chance to be treated like a regular guy. But if he had told Kelly who he was, and taken her to his house and his bed, he would not now be suffering the burning torment of frustration her delectable body had aroused in him.

'Sorry, Kelly. But I will make it up to you tonight, I promise.' His mind was made up: tonight he would tell her the truth. Bending down, he picked up the blanket and the food box in one hand and held the other one out to her.

He glanced down at her silver head, her hand so trustingly in his, and he felt a bit of a bastard. She was a truly lovely girl, both inside and out. He knew she wanted him; she could not hide her reactions. Neither could he, he thought drily, willing his body to subside. But he was not into denial so it would have to be tonight, because tomorrow he was leaving. He had work commitments piling up around his ears, never mind the fact the Bertoni family were returning.

Gianfranco was a sophisticated, experienced man of the world and Kelly, at twenty-one, was obviously no innocent. She was incredibly responsive and went wild in his arms, though sometimes she actually looked surprised at her own reactions. He knew without conceit that he could have had her the first day he'd met her.

He stopped, puzzled for a moment at his own restraint. He was not a man who went in for one-night stands—he usually took a woman out three or four times before taking her to bed. He had to like the woman he was sleeping with, and he certainly liked Kelly. He was looking forward to a new affair as it had been three months since the end of his last relationship. Plus, he wanted to discover if she was as much a gymnast in bed as she was out of it!

His sudden halt about a yard away from the motorbike caught Kelly by surprise and she kept moving. Her hand fell from his, and, turning, she grinned up at him.

'Don't look so worried.' He was watching her as she spoke with an oddly speculative gleam in the dark eyes that met her own. 'We weren't arrested, and it could have been worse,' she offered with a grin. 'At least the chap didn't shoot at us.'

Gianni's lips quirked. He chuckled and then laughed out loud. 'You are so good for me, Kelly. Come on...' And, handing her a helmet, he added, 'Mount up and let's ride.'

'Now, that's an offer few girls could refuse.' She gave him a very sexy wink.

'Get on the bike,' Gianni ordered. 'Before I change my mind,' he teased her with a blatantly salacious grin, his dark eyes sweeping her slender form from the top of her head to her toes. She really was very lovely; she made him feel like a teenager again. She looked like one herself in cut-off denim shorts. It suddenly occurred to him that he'd never seen her wear anything but shorts or trousers. A necessity on a bike, but he could not help wondering what she would look like sleek and groomed in the kind of designer dress his usual girlfriends favoured. He found himself voicing his thoughts. 'Tonight, wear a dress.'

'On a bike? You *are* joking?' Kelly chuckled, swinging one shapely leg over the saddle.

'No, no, I'm not.' Straddling the bike, he glanced back over his shoulder. 'Tonight we will ride in style. I'll collect you at eight in a car.'

Kelly clasped her hands around his waist and hung on tight as he revved up the engine. Usually she wallowed in the warm protection of his huge body as they rode along the road, but not today. Instead her brain ran a hasty inventory of her wardrobe and she realised she had absolutely nothing to wear!

When she heard the doorbell ring Kelly waved goodbye to a frowning Marta and dashed down the marble hall to the entrance door. She was praying Gianni would approve of the pale pink silk-lined chiffon dress that she had bought that afternoon from a sale rack in a very expensive boutique in the town.

Gianni's reaction was all she'd hoped for. His dark eyes widened and an arrested expression crossed his ruggedly attractive face. 'You look absolutely stunning, Kelly.'

'I did as you said. I wore a dress,' Kelly responded softly, her heart swelling with love and pride, her eyes drinking in the sight of him. A pale green shirt fitted perfectly across his broad shoulders, open at the neck to reveal the tanned column of his throat. Cream pleated cotton trousers skimmed his lean hips and long strong legs, and on his feet were brown hide loafers.

She looked back up at his face and her breath caught in her throat. He was so handsome, and somehow different, older than the devil-may-care biker she had fallen in love with.

Gianfranco was silent for a long moment, his dark eyes narrowing assessingly on her face and shapely body. The long silver-blonde hair was swept up on top of her head, revealing a diamond crucifix glinting at her throat. The jewels were genuine. The elegant pink dress and shoes were designer wear. He should know—he had bought enough clothes for females over the years.

His dark brows drew together in a frown. Maybe she knew who he was. Who was fooling whom? he wondered wryly. Tonight she looked older than her twenty-one, a mature, sophisticated lady, and hey, if she liked to play games, all the better; she obviously knew the score.

'Gianni.' Kelly had an uneasy feeling that she had upset him somehow, and she wondered if everyone in love felt this roller-coaster ride between high and low. Her stomach did flip-flops and her pulse raced at the sight of him, but he only had to frown and she was worried sick.

A relieved if slightly cynical smile parted his firm lips.

'Kelly, *cara*.' He drawled the endearment and, taking her arm, added, 'Come on, let's go eat.'

Encouraged by the endearment, and a minute later seated in the passenger seat of a big blue Volvo car, she asked as Gianni slid behind the driving wheel, 'This is a nice car; is it yours?'

'My family's.' Bending over, Gianni pressed a swift, hard kiss on her mouth. 'Don't worry, I have not stolen it,' he quipped.

'I would not dream of thinking such a thing,' Kelly said drolly.

'Of course not.' One dark brow arched sardonically in her direction and they both chuckled, remembering their first meeting.

Kelly's earlier fear was quickly dismissed, and half an hour later, when he took her hand as he helped her out of the car, she looked up with interest at the large grey stone house set in a small clearing surrounded by trees. 'Where are we?' Kelly queried. It did not look like a restaurant. A single window was lit, the light spilling out over a terrace, and there was not a soul in sight.

'I did think of taking you to the most expensive restaurant in the area.' Gianni turned her to face him, and added, 'But I thought of something more private,' he husked in a deeply sensual tone.

The butterflies in Kelly's stomach started a stampede, but she was where she wanted to be, with Gianni, and, lifting her head, she beamed up at him. 'Admit it. You couldn't afford it,' she challenged him teasingly. 'So you decided to break into a house in the woods.'

'Your imagination will get you into trouble one day, sweetheart,' he drawled cynically, but the gleam of laughter in the dark eyes as they met hers belied his cynicism. 'We don't have to break in—I have a key. The house is owned by the company I work for, and I have permission to use it.'

'Oh, so it's empty,' she murmured weakly, and swallowed hard, knowing once she entered the house she was tacitly agreeing to furthering their intimate relationship.

'I'm not going to lie to you, Kelly. I want you; you know that,' he said softly. 'But I promise I will not do anything you don't want me to,' Gianni assured her with a smile. 'Now, come on, dinner is waiting. I was up here earlier and prepared it.'

'You can cook?' she asked as he pushed open the door and with a hand at her back urged her forward into the house.

'I can do anything,' Gianni said arrogantly, and before she knew his intention he had spun her around into his arms and kissed her long and hard. When he finally lifted his head her eyes, wide and worshipping, clung to his.

'We had better eat,' he said roughly, 'while we still can.'

Kelly knew exactly what he meant. Her hunger for him was growing by the second. She did not know this sensual, needy woman she had become with Gianni. But her mind was made up—she was going to take the chance and find out...

They ate out on the terrace by candle light. Gianni was a marvellous host, but Kelly had to laugh at the food.

'You call that cooking?' she jibed as she forked the last mouthful of potato salad into her mouth. He had served melon with Parma ham, followed by prawns with salad, then cold cuts of meat with more salad. 'There was not a single dish that needed cooking, you fraud. I bet you simply bought the lot in the delicatessen in town.'

'Maybe so, but it worked—I needed to get you alone,' he drawled with a lascivious grin, and filled her glass with white wine yet again.

She lifted laughing blue eyes to his. 'You are incorrigible.'

'I know.' His brown eyes danced with devilment as they met hers, and for a moment the shared humour united them, but subtly the mood changed and their eyes meshed. 'Kelly,' Gianni murmured her name, 'we don't have much time left; your employer is back tomorrow and I have to go to Genoa; I will be away for a few days.'

Her heart sank. 'You're going away.' Their holiday idyll was at an end, but it did not mean their relationship had to end, she told herself staunchly.

'It will be at least a week before we can see each other again.' He reached out to her, his hands palm up on the table. 'Shall we go inside?'

Her heart lifted: he did intend seeing her again. She glanced up into his deep brown eyes, and what she saw there made her pulse race. She knew all evening had been leading to this moment. They had laughed and joked, but the underlining sexual tension had been growing stronger and stronger. She knew what he was offering, and she knew if she took his hands there would be no going back.

She placed her glass on the table, and put her hands in his.

Gianni lifted them both to his mouth, pressing a soft kiss to the centre of each palm before rising to his feet.

Feeling Kelly tremble, Gianni pulled her up and into his arms. She was so soft, so warm, so his! he thought triumphantly as he claimed her lush, pouting lips with his own.

'Gianni,' she moaned his name, her slender body quivering with a need, a want she could not control. She looked up into his night-dark eyes and knew it was the same for him.

'Yes, my sweet Kelly,' he husked as he lifted her off her feet and carried her up the stairs to the bedroom, all the time pressing brief kisses to her lips, her cheek, her eyes, nuzzling the curve of her neck.

'*Dio!* Kelly, you have no idea how much I ache for you,' he groaned, lowering her down the long length of his body and holding her slightly away from him. 'I don't think I can wait any longer.' He caught her shoulders and eased the straps of her dress down over her arms. His brilliant brown eyes holding hers, she felt the gentle stroke of his fingers on her bare flesh right through to her bones.

'I want to see you naked.' He slid the dress down her body to pool at her feet.

Standing before him in tiny lacy briefs, Kelly shuddered as his hands slid back up her hips and shaped the indentation of her waist, and watched as his dark eyes dropped to savour the glory of her near-naked body. His hands tightened around her waist. The bones of his face were taut with passion and for the briefest second she was afraid.

He sensed her fear, and loosened his hold. His hands skimmed over the silk slide of her skin to her breasts. 'You are incredible, so responsive, so beautiful.' Her skin was as pale as ivory, her body toned to perfection, with high full breasts tipped with delicate rosebuds. His body hardened to steel, and want raced through him like a tidal wave. 'No woman has ever affected me the way you do, Kelly.' He bent his head towards her, his breath brushing her lips. 'But if you want me to stop, say so now,' he murmured, and kissed her lightly. He did not trust himself to do more.

Kelly swayed into him, her lips parting on a trembling sigh, her fingers reaching for his shirt buttons. 'I don't want you to stop,' she whispered against his mouth. 'Not ever.'

Their mouths met in a hungry, ravishing kiss that blanked every doubt from her mind—all she could think, feel and taste was Gianni. His head lifted and he eased her away from him. She followed his movements with longing in her brilliant sapphire eyes, and in seconds Gianni was naked.

Fascination kept her still, her eyes roaming over his body in wonder. He was magnificent, like a sculptured god to her innocent gaze. She dragged a breath into her air-starved lungs and caught that musky fragrance of masculine arousal. She saw his sex surging from the curling black nest of his groin, and wild colour flooded over every inch of her skin.

Gianni, reaching out for her, hesitated for a second and stepped back, his dark eyes narrowing. 'You're blushing as though you had never seen a naked man before.'

'The curse of the McKenzies, my father always said. He was ginger-haired and always blushed.' She was babbling, she knew, but without Gianni's touch to reassure her she suddenly felt exposed. 'My mother suffered from the same affliction, and I take after both my parents.'

'Hush.' Gianni silenced her ramblings by drawing her into his arms. 'I like it,' he said, and quite unexpectedly he felt rotten. Kelly knew next to nothing about him, not even his real name. He must tell her.

'And I like you,' Kelly murmured as he held her close to his naked body. She was drowning in a million sensations. She did not care that the light was still on; in fact, she knew the picture of him in all his nudity would live with her to her dying day. She stroked her slender hands up his spine, down over his buttocks. He felt like satin and steel, hot and hard, and she ached to know every inch of him.

Gianni's great body shuddered as her small hot hand slid like silk up his spine. He swung her up into his arms and carried her to the bed, dropped her down on it.

Breathless, she smiled up at him, a slow, soft curve of her incredibly sexy mouth. Her sapphire-blue eyes, shining like stars, met his, and she reached two slender arms out to him.

'My full...' Name, he was going to say, but her lithe naked body spread on the bed was too much. '*Dio, sì*, Kelly,' he said in a strangled voice. It could wait, but he couldn't, and he joined her on the bed.

Her heart racing, Kelly curved her hands around his shoulders, letting her fingers curl into the soft black hair at the nape of his neck, urging him down to her. 'Yes,' she breathed. A tremulous little gasp caught in her throat, and anticipation made her moan out loud as he covered her face with tiny kisses before finally claiming her mouth. She felt his kiss, the stroke of his hand down to cup the fullness of her breast in every cell in her body. Excitement surged through her, making her arch against him with a soft whimper of need. Her fingers dug into his skin as he lowered his head, trailing a fiery line of kisses down her throat to her breast, his mouth closing over one hard tip, suckling and tasting, until she cried out with pleasure.

With a wantonness that amazed her, her body responded to his every touch. He was a magnificent male animal, power and virility in every line of his huge body. He nudged her legs apart with one of his own, and she gasped as his long fingers delved between her thighs, but her legs moved wider, welcoming the intimate caress.

Her hands slipped down to clutch his hips, one small hand stroking across his thigh, revelling in the different textures of skin and soft curling body hair, and tentatively to the core of his manhood.

Gianni instantly reared back. 'Kelly,' he grated, his massive chest heaving. He wanted to take it slowly. He wanted it to be good for her, the best ever. He did not ask himself why.

'Don't stop,' Kelly begged, her blue eyes, dark with need, fixed on his hard face. 'Please, please,' she moaned.

Gianni slid his hands beneath her hips and lifted her to him. His need for her sang in his blood, raced through his veins. There was a roaring in his ears and any notion of taking it slowly was obliterated.

With one swift thrust he entered her, sheathing himself inside her. Kelly cried out as a fierce pain ripped through her. For a second Gianni froze, but before she could react to the pain with a low groan he surged into the hot, sleek centre of her again and again, and slowly the pain subsided. Euphoria took over as he drove her higher and higher to some destination she had only ever dreamed about.

Afterwards Kelly wrapped her arms around his neck, hugging his great body, relishing his weight on her as the sounds of their frantic breathing became regulated. She could not find the words to describe how he made her feel. He had captured her heart and soul. 'I love you,' she sighed, and with a murmur of pleasure kissed his sweat-slicked shoulder, still wanting more.

Gianni said something harsh and guttural in Italian and tore himself from her arms and leapt off the bed. 'You were a virgin,' he grated incredulously, his dark eyes narrowing down to where she lay naked on the bed. 'Why the hell did you not tell me?' he demanded with barely contained rage. He could not believe he had lost control so totally *and* maybe fallen for the oldest trick in the book…

CHAPTER THREE

'I NEVER thought,' she murmured, her new-found euphoria dwindling at the repressed fury in his tone. Towering over her, the lover of a moment ago was gone, and in his place was a furious naked man; his hard eyes clashed with hers and the dark menace of his expression made her inwardly wince. Kelly did not understand what she had done wrong. Her mouth dried, and she dampened her top lip with her tongue, tearing her gaze away from the violence in his.

'You never thought!' snorted Gianni, shaking his dark head in disgust.

Kelly had no defence. She could not help having been a virgin, and it had never entered her head to mention the fact. How naïve could one get? she thought, feeling sick with a mixture of embarrassment and humiliation. 'Obviously I made a mistake,' she said in a flat little voice, forcing the words past trembling lips; suddenly she quite desperately wanted to cry.

'I certainly did,' he muttered between clenched teeth as he began to pull on his clothes. 'A virgin.' His black brows drew together in a frown as he surveyed her slender body spread-eagled on the bed where he had left her, the blush of passion tinting her pale skin. 'Cover yourself, for God's sake!'

The electric light that she had not objected to before now seemed to be fixed like a spotlight on her naked body. Jerking up into a sitting position, she grabbed the sheet and tugged it up under her chin. 'I'm sorry.' But she was not apologising to him, she was sorry for herself—his reaction had turned what she had thought was a wonderful experience into something shoddy and shameful.

Kelly saw it all clearly now. Gianni had been looking for a holiday fling, and she, poor fool that she was, had thought it was love, the real thing...

'Sorry. You're sorry!' Gianni snarled. 'What about me? Is it too much to hope you are on the Pill, or can I expect a paternity suit in a few months' time?'

As soon as the words left his mouth he knew he was being cruelly unfair. He should have used protection. But he had been so out of his head with wanting Kelly that for the first time in his life he had forgotten. He had lost control, and not only that, he thought, as his dark eyes, bright and hard as jet, raked over her huddled figure on the bed: he had taken her virginity and not even satisfied Kelly sexually, something else he never failed to do with his usual lady-friends. It was a massive blow to his ego. But then, he had known the moment he'd set eyes on her she would drive him crazy, and she had. He needed to think, and think hard, and he could not do it with Kelly sitting like a broken doll on the bed.

'Sorry, Kelly—' he reached out a hand to her '—I should not have said that.' Whether she was a clever little fortune-hunter or not, she did not deserve his anger.

Pregnant! Paternity! While she had thought love, he had been counting costs. All the colour drained from her skin, and cold beads of sweat broke out across her upper lip; she had the horrible conviction she had just made the biggest mistake of her life. How could she have been such a gullible, careless fool? Galvanised into action by his outstretched hand, Kelly knocked it away and shot out of the other side of the bed. Wrapping the sheet around her shivering body, she raised stormy eyes to his across the wide expanse of the bed, anger, hot and hard, coming to her rescue.

'Oh, please, don't apologise; you could not possibly be as sorry as I am.' Ignoring him completely, she set about picking up her clothes.

He caught up with her as she was heading for the door. 'Wait.' His hands grasped one of hers and spun her around to face him.

'What for? A repeat performance—I don't think so,' she shot back, fighting down a reckless impulse to fling herself in his arms and cry her eyes out. She was angry and ashamed, and physically sore, and with her dream of love shattered. But Kelly was a quick learner.

'No.' His mouth compressed into a humourless smile. 'I am not a complete monster, Kelly, though I guess at this minute you will have trouble believing that. Go ahead and get dressed, and then we will talk.' And before she could stop him she was abruptly hauled hard against his lean body and he kissed her again.

The moment his lips touched hers, the familiar longing swept like wildfire through her veins, but just before she capitulated to the wicked temptation of his mouth he pushed her lightly away. His hooded dark eyes were guarded as he looked down at her. 'The bathroom is over there.' He indicated the door with a pointed finger, and he had the gall to pretend to smile with a twist of his lips, but the humour never reached his eyes.

Embarrassed yet again by her traitorous body's response, she blushed scarlet and darted into the bathroom. Five minutes later, washed and dressed and standing before the vanity mirror, she raked her hands through the tangled mass of her hair, trying to restore it to some order. The pins she'd used had vanished in the bed. She bit her bottom lip to stop herself crying. What should have been the most perfect night of her life had turned into the worst.

A rap on the door made her jump. 'Kelly, are you OK?' The caring note in his rich, deep voice was like rubbing salt in an open wound.

Kelly took a deep breath and straightened her slender shoulders, a cynical little smile curving her bruised lips. 'Just coming,' she carolled. No way was she going to let him see how much he had hurt her. But it wasn't easy.

Walking into the bedroom, she was struck anew by the fierce sexual hunger she had felt from the first moment she had laid eyes on him. It wasn't fair. She almost groaned. He was standing by the door, his dark eyes fixed broodingly on his own large hand curved around the handle. The terrible compulsion to stare was almost uncontrollable. His chiselled profile, with the endearing crook in the nose, the high cheekbones and the firm, sensuous mouth, all added up to one staggeringly handsome man. A man whose long, lithe body looked poised for flight. Her stomach clenched, her hunger for him undiminished even now, when he had made it blatantly obvious he no longer wanted her. Probably never had.

Where is your pride, girl? Kelly asked herself, and, straightening her shoulders, her long lashes half-lowered over her too vulnerable eyes, she rubbed damp palms down her slender hips and walked towards him.

'I'll take you home,' Gianni said in a level voice, not looking at her.

They hadn't been more than ten silent minutes in the car when the tension beating on Kelly's nerves began to give her a terrible headache. She glanced sideways at Gianni through the long length of her lashes. His dark features were calmly composed, as though he hadn't a care in the world. But then, he hadn't, unless she was even more naïve than she thought. She was pretty certain he had got some physical satisfaction from the evening. Even if she'd been inadequate in other ways.

'You never answered my question.'

Gianni's disembodied voice seemed to attack her from the darkness. She twisted her head around. 'What question?'

'Are you on the Pill or is there a chance you might be pregnant?' He slanted her a brief glance, one black brow arching enquiringly.

'No, and highly unlikely,' she said flatly, taking a deep, shaky breath and surreptitiously crossing her fingers.

A large hand landed on her thigh, and she flinched. 'I will take care of you, Kelly, if the need arises,' he said. His tone implied that he would rather it didn't.

Furiously she knocked his hand off her leg, colour staining her cheeks, and she blessed the darkness. 'There will be no need. I can take care of myself.'

'As you did tonight?' Gianni grated harshly.

'Just shut up and drive,' Kelly snapped, not prepared to argue.

The car swung alongside the kerb outside the iron gates; clearly choosing not to drive in, Gianni turned in his seat. He looked at her slender body curled into the corner of the passenger seat, as far away from him as she could get. With her face scrubbed free of make-up, and her silver hair hanging loose around her shoulders, she looked so young, and guilt hit him like a punch to the stomach. 'I didn't mean to hurt you tonight.' He had the totally alien desire to protect her.

Tears ached at the backs of Kelly's eyes. 'You didn't,' she managed to say, and, fumbling with her seatbelt, she avoided his knowing gaze.

'I did and I am sorry. But I was surprised. I thought...'

'You thought I was an easy lay—the English tourist; I know the reputation,' she said scathingly, turning her back on him and trying to open the door. She had to get away before she broke down and bawled her eyes out. Her delicately arched brows drew together in fierce concentration. How the hell did the door open? And how the hell had she allowed herself to act so bloody dumb?

'No, no, never that.' Gianni reached out for her with a half-groan. 'You don't understand, Kelly. I was amazed you were innocent, and shock made me shout at you.' He linked confident arms around her tense body and eased her around to face him. 'But I don't want us to end like this.' He smoothed a few strands of pale hair from her creased brow.

Held against his hard, lithe body, with his brilliant gaze riveted to hers, dimly she understood how a bird must feel, mesmerised by the predatory eyes of a great cat.

'You don't?' she asked, hardly daring to hope. His brown eyes were gleaming with what actually looked like remorse. Her skin prickled with sudden heat, and Gianni's hand dropped lower, to tangle in a whole handful of her silken hair and twist it around his fingers, his dark, compelling gaze never leaving hers. Her tongue snaked out to moisten her dry lips.

'No.' His eyes dropped to the lush fullness of her damp lips, and, bending his head, he gently brushed them with his. He touched her and she melted; it was that basic, Kelly realised with a low groan.

Gianni lifted his head and stared down into her wary blue eyes; he knew he had put the suspicion there and hated himself for it. He lifted a finger and pressed it against the pulse that beat madly in her neck. 'This chemistry between us is more than I believed possible between a man and woman. Tonight I was a fool. In the urgency of passion I took what should have been a special gift, like the thief you once called me. I was angrier with myself than you. But the next time I swear will be perfect.'

Kelly heard what he was saying and suddenly she understood. This wonderful, vulnerable man had been angry because he thought he had not pleased her. The love in her heart burst into flame all over again. 'Oh, Gianni, any time I am with you is perfect,' she said impulsively, and she felt as if the weight of the world had been lifted from her shoulders.

His cynical mind thought, Flattery, or fact? He didn't know, but he was going to take the chance—though he would put off telling her who he was just yet. He smiled, a slow, sexy curve of his firm lips, half-humorous and half-cynical. She could no more hide her feelings than fly; her expressive eyes gave her away or she was a great actress, he thought just before he lowered his head to claim her mouth once more.

'And this is Andrea, running after the stray cats at the Coliseum.' Judy Bertoni, her employer, handed Kelly yet another photograph.

They were sitting side by side on the sofa in the salon, sharing a bottle of white wine. Andrea was safely tucked up in bed, and Signor Bertoni was out at the sailing club.

Kelly grinned at Judy. 'You seem to have had a great time in Rome, and you managed to look after Andrea with no bother at all. I feel quite superfluous.'

'The in-laws were impressed, but your help was invaluable.' Judy, a tall, elegant brunette, had been a model before she married, and was not the most hands-on mother in the world.

'I wasn't there,' Kelly reminded her with a grin.

'I know.' Judy smiled a very self-satisfied smirk. 'But

Carlo realised the difference. The weeks we have been here with you to help, he has had a lot more…attention from me, shall we say?' she declared archly. 'In Rome I made sure he noticed the difference, with Andrea occupying most of my time and energy.' She winked at Kelly. 'The result being, when we return to England he is going to employ a full-time nanny. I can't think why I didn't think of doing it before.'

Kelly had to laugh. 'I think your poor husband hasn't got a chance.' When it came to getting what she wanted Judy was a master of the art. Kelly knew for a fact she had pursued Carlo Bertoni quite deliberately, determined to marry him. Judy had confided as much. Carlo Bertoni was a wealthy man and ran the British branch of the family import and export buisness. He was also a rather old-fashioned, traditional Italian male. His mother had never employed a nanny to look after him and he saw no reason why his wife could not look after their child herself.

'Anyway, enough about me,' Judy said, and, refilling the two glasses of wine on the table in front of them, she lifted her glass to her lips and surveyed Kelly through slightly narrowed eyes. 'Marta tells me you have succumbed to the Italian male's charm and found yourself a boyfriend. Come on, spill the beans. Where did you meet? Who is he? What does he do?'

It was a new experience for Kelly, having another woman to talk to, and suddenly she found herself telling Judy all about Gianni. 'I met him here last week. He is gorgeous, tall, dark and handsome, and he works at the harbour and lives in the old town.'

'Oh, no!' Judy exclaimed. 'You've fallen for one of the locals. For heaven's sake, Kelly, you can do much better for yourself than some manual worker.'

Kelly stiffened at Judy's derogatory comment. 'You

don't understand; we are in love,' she defended. For her it was true, and on Friday night when she had finally left Gianni she had been convinced he loved her too. He had arranged to telephone her on Monday and they were to meet next Friday at a small *trattoria* they had visited before.

'Love!' Judy laughed. 'Take my advice, Kelly—if you must have a bit of rough, make sure you are protected.'

'Thanks very much,' Kelly drawled sarcastically, her anger rising at Judy's summary dismissal of Gianni. But in her position as employee she could not really argue with Judy. If Judy had a fault she was a bit of a snob. Biting her lip to stop herself saying something she might regret, Kelly lifted her glass and took a long swallow of wine.

Judy had not even noticed the sarcasm in Kelly's response. 'My pleasure.' She smiled briefly at Kelly, no longer interested, and, glancing at the slim gold Rolex on her wrist, she sighed, picked up the remote control and switched on the television.

So what if Gianni did have calluses on his hands and worked hard for a living? Did that make him any less a man? No, Kelly thought, a dreamy, reminiscent smile curving her full lips, a vivid mental image of his big naked bronzed body filling her mind. She could barely wait until Friday; she missed him so much.

'I wonder where Carlo has got to...he is very late.' Judy's voice impinged on her musings, and at that moment the door opened and in walked Carlo Bertoni.

'Oh, my God! What's happened?' Judy leapt to her feet and dashed to her husband's side.

Kelly's eyes widened like saucers at the picture her employer presented. One arm was in a sling, and a swath of bandages circled his head. His usually tanned face looked grey, and it was obvious he was in some pain.

Within minutes the whole story was revealed. He had been hit by the boom of his yacht, fallen and broken his arm. He had been to the hospital, had an X-ray and five stitches in his head, and his arm put in plaster. He insisted his injuries were not half as bad as the fact he would now miss the big race next week. Then Judy reminded him it was the last night of the open-air opera in Verona tomorrow night and they had VIP seats.

The next day Carlo Bertoni flatly refused to go to the opera. His head was aching and he insisted he would stay at home with Andrea, and Kelly should go in his place. Judy was not pleased but, as she would not miss it for the world because it was a big social occasion, she agreed.

Which was why Kelly was dressed in the pink chiffon dress and, in her matching beaded cardigan, was happily following Judy into the ancient arena at nine that night.

It was huge. Right in the centre of the floor in front of the orchestra pit, where the stage had been erected, was a square area roped off and filled with white chairs. Judy explained as they slid into their seats that these were the VIP seats. The grey chairs rising in row upon row beyond were numbered seats, and then the ancient stone slabs that rose in circle upon circle to the very top of the arena were the un-numbered seats.

With the starlit blackness of the night sky for a roof, the atmosphere was electric as everyone waited for the opera to start. Kelly's head swivelled around in awed wonder at her surroundings; there was hardly a seat left except for a few in front of them. 'This is incredible.' She turned to Judy but her companion was watching the last few people arrive.

'Now *that* is what I call incredible.' Judy shot her a sidelong glance. 'Isn't he the most devastatingly attractive man you have ever seen?'

Following the direction of her employer's gaze, Kelly blinked and jerked upright in her seat.

'Count Gianfranco Maldini, *the* most eligible bachelor in Europe, possibly the world. Will you look at him, Kelly? The man has it all. Style, breeding, handsome as the devil, and filthy rich. He is enough to make a happily married woman drool.'

Kelly was looking, but she could not believe her eyes. The man walking to the seats in front of them was the epitome of sartorial elegance. A perfectly tailored dark suit fitted his broad-shouldered long-bodied frame to perfection, the brilliant white shirt that accompanied it showing exactly the right amount of cuff and the glint of a gold cuff-link beneath the jacket sleeve.

She blinked and blinked again. She shook her head. No, it couldn't be... 'Who did you say it was?' She was totally confused. The man was the spitting image of Gianni, but with subtle differences. This man looked older; his features were the same, but the laughter that sparkled in Gianni's eyes was not evident in this man's cold, arrogant features.

Judy shot her an excited glance. 'Count Gianfranco Maldini. The family estate is in Lombardy, but he has vast holdings all over the place. Carlo knows him and he is hoping to do a deal importing the wine from the Bardolino vineyard the Count owns into England.'

Kelly squeezed her eyes shut, willing the image of the man to go away. She opened her eyes again, and a dreadful fear made the blood drain from her face. The stunningly handsome man not five feet away from her even had the same crook in his nose as her Gianni, but it could not be...

'What did you say his first name was?' Kelly asked, still not prepared to believe it.

'Gianfranco.'

'But isn't that two names?' She was still denying the truth before her very eyes.

'No. Think about it. The pope is called Gianpaulo; Giancarlo, Gianluca—they are all quite popular names. Especially in the kind of aristocratic family Gianfranco Maldini belongs to,' Judy whispered to her in an aside, and then, to Kelly's horror, Judy rose and called something in Italian to the man.

Nausea rose up Kelly's throat like bile. She could not deny the evidence of her own eyes any longer. It was Gianni, her Gianni, but not as she had ever seen him. Tall and sophisticated, and with his unruly curls slicked back from his broad brow, he looked superb. Strikingly handsome, every inch the sophisticated aristocrat his title proved him to be.

The taste of bitter humiliation in her mouth, Kelly tried to huddle down in her seat, her heart squeezing in anguish. He had lied to her, made a complete fool of her, and with each second that passed she died a little more inside.

'And this is Kelly McKenzie, my nanny. Kelly.' Judy's voice rose, and Kelly had no choice but to get to her feet and be introduced to Count Maldini.

'Ah, Kelly.' His dark eyes smiled down at her, and she just knew he was going to say he had met her already.

Pride alone made her jump in and stick out her hand. 'A pleasure to meet you, Count Maldini.' It was bad enough she had made a fool of herself over this man, but no way did she want her stupidity revealed to Judy Bertoni, or anyone else. Her hand was swallowed up in his and he gave her a quizzical look, before lifting her hand and pressing it to his mouth. She felt the electric sensation right down to her toes, and he knew, the devil, and his black eyes were laughing down at her in secret mirth at her charade. 'How do you like our country?' he asked politely.

She wrenched her hand from his. 'The country is nice.' She did not know how she got the words out. She was in shock, but her ordeal was not over, as with impeccable manners he introduced the two women who accompanied him.

His mother, a silver-haired lady who had to be over sixty but looked much younger, gave Kelly one brief glance down her elegant nose and murmured the appropriate response. The other woman was thirty-ish, beautiful and superbly dressed. She had one hand resting on the count's sleeve, and the other she held out to Kelly. Apparently, she was his sister-in-law, Olivia Maldini.

'This must be a great treat for a nanny,' Olivia added to her conventional greeting, her cold dark eyes skimming over Kelly and a patronising smile curving her rather thin lips.

'You could say that,' Kelly snapped back, suddenly seeing red and a few other colours beside. The shock that had kept her frozen for so long was evaporating and in its place was a towering rage. 'I am not really a nanny. I finished university in June and I am just filling in for the summer before I begin my career as a research chemist for the government in October.' Blue eyes flashing angrily, she glanced back up at Gianni—no, not Gianni, she reminded herself, but Count Gianfranco Maldini. The arrogance, the conniving, lying cheek of the man was unbelievable.

'I think it is so important to be truthful about such things straight away, to avoid any misconceptions later. Don't you agree, Count Maldini?' Kelly drawled his name as she asked the question in a voice laced with bitter sarcasm. She was not having these tinpot aristocrats patronising her.

His tanned face flushed dark with embarrassment, or was it rage? For a second she thought she had gone too far. His brown eyes narrowed on her face, hard as jet, but when he spoke he was all suave charm. 'Yes, of course, Kelly, you are right.'

Out of the corner of her eye she saw Judy flash her an angry look before saying something to Olivia in Italian. Probably apologising for her nanny's bad manners, Kelly thought as rage bubbled inside her.

'But in some situations there is no time for the truth to be heard.' Gianfranco's mouth twisted in a wry self-mocking smile at her obvious anger.

What had he expected? He had been so surprised to see Kelly that he had gone along with her obvious wish to pretend she did not know him. A horrendous mistake; he should have admitted straight away he knew her. Hell! Who was he kidding? He should have told her from the outset who he really was, certainly before he had taken her to bed... It was hardly surprising she was furious. But now was not the time or the place to try and explain.

'Excuse us, we have to take our seats now, but perhaps later...' Gianfranco addressed his words to Judy Bertoni '...you and Kelly would like to join us for a late meal?'

Kelly stiffened and, freed from the tension of his dark gaze, she shivered at the thought of spending one more moment in his company. She saw Judy open her mouth and accept, and her worst fear was realised.

There was no way Kelly could eat and drink with this man. The more she looked at him, the more she realised the depths of his deception. The aura of dynamic power and status was glaringly evident. This man was a stranger to her...

She recalled the first day, when he had introduced himself as Gianfranco and she had called him Signor Franco. A laugh and a simple explanation and the last week would never have happened.

Kelly took a deep breath, reminding herself wryly that

she was an adult woman and not a stupid teenager any more. The signs had been there for her to see; the fact that love had blinded her was really her own fault. She lifted her head and discovered to her amazement that rescue had come from the most unexpected source.

'Olivia is right.' Judy was talking to Count Maldini. 'Much as we would have enjoyed joining your party later, I must refuse. My husband is still in great pain. But as he insisted I did not miss the gala tonight, the least I can do is get back to his side as quickly as possible.'

'But of course,' Count Maldini agreed. 'Another time, perhaps.'

Suddenly everyone was making for his or her seat, and Kelly sank back down in her own as the orchestra began to tune up.

'Bitch,' Judy whispered in an aside to Kelly.

'What?' Kelly asked. 'What did I...?'

'No, not you, silly! Olivia Maldini. I told her about Carlo's accident and she immediately implied I should be at home looking after him—her way of making sure I refused the invitation to join their party. Ever since her husband died three years ago...' Judy flashed Kelly an old-fashioned glance '...it has been rumoured she would not be averse to marrying his younger brother. She obviously saw you and me as competition. Mind you, I don't think she will succeed. Gianfranco dates some of...a lot of,' she amended with a knowing grin, 'the most beautiful women in the world. I can't see him settling for one alone, and, though his sister-in-law is OK, she is nothing special.'

With a kind of sick fascination Kelly watched as Gianfranco's party took their seats in the front row. She was numb; she hardly dared breathe because she knew the pain was waiting for her...

Afterwards Kelly did not remember a single scene from the opera *Don Giovanni*.

She heard Judy's voice as if from a distance.

'Hurry, Kelly. We might catch the count on the way out. I want to invite him to dinner. It might help Carlo clinch his business deal with the man.' Judy leapt to her feet.

Kelly had no desire ever to speak to the count again, and in a desperate attempt to delay she deliberately dropped her purse on the floor. Ducking down, she scraped around on the floor, pretending she had lost something, and when she finally straightened up the Maldini party had left and Judy was spitting nails.

Kelly thought her ordeal was over, but no such luck. By the time they got back to the villa Judy had got over her bad temper, and, after discovering her husband was already in bed and asleep, insisted Kelly share a nightcap with her. She proceeded to regale Kelly with every last bit of information she knew about the count.

'Actually, I think I still have the magazine from last year when the count allowed them to do a ten-page spread on his lifestyle. But only on condition they made a large donation to a town on the edge of the River Poe that was almost buried in a landslide.'

It was pure torture for Kelly. She drained her glass of wine, and for the first time in her life wished she could drink a whole bottle and block out the horror of the evening.

But when Judy returned, and spread a well-known Italian magazine on the table and began pointing out the various pictures, it got even worse. Kelly looked at the pictures with sick humiliation almost choking her.

The enormous family home in the heart of the countryside, the New York and the Rome apartments, the ocean-going yacht at Genoa harbour. But what finally broke

Kelly's heart was the picture of what was called a hunting lodge on a hillside above Lake Garda.

She recognised it. The house where he had taken her last Friday—the house he had told her belonged to the company he worked for. As if that was not enough to convince her, the last picture was of Gianni sitting astride his motor bike, apparently talking to a man with a gun bent over his arm—the security guard.

Her whole body clenched in pain, nausea knotting her stomach. The same man who had found them almost naked at the lakeside last week; the same man Gianni had spoken to. While she had thought they were in trouble for trespassing Gianni must have been laughing like a drain at how easily he had fooled her.

'Are you all right?' Judy asked, suddenly noticing Kelly's long silence.

'I feel a bit sick; probably the wine. I think I'll go to bed.' And she ran.

CHAPTER FOUR

Sick at heart, Kelly stripped off her clothes and stepped into the shower. She turned the water on and stood under the soothing spray, her tears mingling with the water. God, what a disaster of a night! A disaster of a week!

She should have known meeting the man of her dreams was too good to be true.

She should have gone with her first impression on seeing Gianni. A man up to no good. She had got that right! He was a lying, deceitful pig.

Kelly sighed. Knowing the truth did not make the pain go away. It hurt, it really hurt, and she had no one to blame but herself. She had allowed herself to succumb to his surface looks and charm, while he had simply been slumming it for a few days. No wonder he had been horrified when he'd discovered she was a virgin and the possibility of pregnancy was a real threat. His anger at the time, and his crack about a paternity suit, made perfect sense now. If or when Count Maldini married it would be to some suitably wealthy well-connected Italian girl, not some unknown orphan like Kelly.

Turning off the shower, she stepped out and took a large towel off the rail, and briskly rubbed herself dry. She was bone tired, her head ached, and all she wanted to do was sleep. She dropped the towel on the floor and walked into the bedroom. She slipped, naked, into bed. But sleep was a long time in coming.

Every time she closed her eyes she saw the image of Gianni... No, not Gianni...Count Gianfranco Maldini, she kept reminding herself, and when she had reminded herself for the hundredth time of his cruel deceit she finally cried herself to sleep.

At seven the following morning a wide-awake, laughing Andrea jumped on Kelly's bed. Bleary-eyed, she surveyed the little boy, and with a wry smile dragged herself out of bed. Experience told her that his parents would not be up for an hour or so yet, and after bathing and dressing Andrea and herself she made her way downstairs to the kitchen.

Fifteen minutes later she sat at the table watching Andrea with an indulgent smile. He was a lovely little boy who, after devouring a bowl of cereal and a glass of orange juice, was intent on tearing a bread roll into the shape of some mythical beast as shown on the cereal packet. His innocent enjoyment of something so simple put her own problems into some kind of perspective.

So she had allowed herself to be sweet-talked into bed by a devious man out for a bit of fun. She was not the first woman in the world to fall for the charms of a sophisticated male on the make, and she would certainly not be the last. Chalk it up to experience and get on with life, she told herself firmly.

Picking up her coffee-cup, she drained it and placed it back on the table. There was about as much chance of Count Gianfranco Maldini ringing her as the Pope marrying, she thought wryly. But in that she was to be proved wrong...

'Right, young man.' She rose to her feet. 'How about...?' But the ringing of the telephone prevented her continuing. 'OK, Andrea, stay there a minute.' Crossing the room to the wall-mounted telephone, she lifted the receiver to her ear.

'*Pronto.*' She gave the conventional greeting.

'Kelly? Kelly, is that you?' There was no mistaking the rich, deep tone of Gianfranco Maldini.

Shock kept her silent for a moment, and her first thought was to hang up, but then anger came to her aid. 'Yes,' she snapped. 'Who is it calling, please, and to whom do you wish to speak?' she asked facetiously.

'Gianfranco, and to you, of course,' his deep voice drawled huskily. 'Look, Kelly, I can understand why you are angry, but please believe me, I meant to tell you—'

'At least you are using your real name,' she cut in bitterly. 'I suppose I should be grateful, but you know, for some strange reason I am not. It might have something to do with the fact I went to bed with a stranger, or maybe just an old-fashioned idea of believing in the truth—something you obviously know nothing about.' Her knuckles gleamed white on the hand that gripped the receiver. She was furious, and amazed he had the nerve to call her.

'Listen to me, Kelly,' Gianfranco demanded harshly; her last crack was an insult he would not accept. No one had ever questioned his honesty before. 'I never had any intention to deceive you. The first day we met I tried to tell you my name and you, in your usual manner, leapt in with "Hello, Signor Franco." You jump to conclusions like a bull at a gate.'

'Oh, I see! So it is my fault. In a whole week you could not get around to telling me you were not a port worker but Count Gianfranco Maldini. I wonder why? Could it possibly be because you were ashamed of mixing with ordinary people, you arrogant snob?' She was on a roll. From the minute last night when she had discovered who her so-called boyfriend really was, she had swung between hurt and humiliation, but now she was just plain angry. 'Suddenly all the little out-of-the-way places you took me make perfect sense. And of course how could I forget your horror that I was not some vastly experienced woman? And your desperate worry I might slap a paternity suit on you.'

'No,' he snapped. 'Now stop right there.' The sheer force of his voice in her ear made Kelly do just that. 'I am trying to be reasonable, but you are not making it easy for me. I apologise for misleading you about my name, but that is all I apologise for. Last night I was quite prepared to acknowledge we were friends, but you jumped in again and made it very obvious you did not want me to. I followed your lead because I thought that was what you wanted.'

He was right, but the 'friend' rankled. 'Maybe so. But it does not alter the fact you deceived me about who you really were.' She had to battle to retain her anger as the sound of his voice alone made her go weak at the knees.

'Maybe, but I am the same Gianni you dated, the same Gianni who wants to see you again on Friday.'

He still wanted to see her; the thought floored her for a moment. 'But you're a count.'

'So now who is being the snob?' Gianfranco drawled mockingly. 'If I don't care, why should you?'

A glimmer of hope flickered in her heart, and for a second she considered the possibility. Then common sense prevailed.

'Kelly? Kelly, are you still there?' Gianfranco asked urgently.

'Yes,' she responded, hardening her heart against him. 'And where are you calling from?' she demanded in a tone laced with sarcasm. 'Genoa—isn't that where you were supposed to be visiting? Yet I could have sworn I saw you in Verona last night.'

'Sarcasm does not become you, Kelly. I know I made a mistake; when I see you again I will explain everything. But I can't talk now. I have a flight to catch to New York, a flight I delayed for a week to be with you. Surely that must count for something?' Gianfranco Maldini could not believe what he was saying. He was virtually pleading with the girl for a date.

'Then don't let me delay you any further.' It was no good prolonging the agony; Judy had told her about his countless girlfriends, and, even if she could fit into his lifestyle, Kelly did not want to. Eventually she wanted marriage and a husband, not to be a rich man's plaything for a few weeks.

Gianfranco cleared his throat. 'Will you still meet me on Friday as we arranged?' And he held his breath as he waited for her answer.

'No,' Kelly said flatly. 'The more I think about it I realise that last Friday was a disaster. Personally, I am going to put it down to experience and forget we ever met; I suggest you do the same.' She glanced across at Andrea; he had put down the bread and was wriggling uncomfortably in his high chair.

'*Dio!* Kelly?' Gianfranco's patience snapped. His ego had taken enough bruising from this woman, and it did not help to be reminded he'd been a failure in bed. 'You be there on Friday, or I will be around at Bertoni's to get you. Understand?' he shouted. He was not used to having his commands disobeyed.

Andrea was watching her with an open mouth and worried brown eyes; he had never heard her angry before, and, though she doubted he understood the words, he could sense something was wrong, and he did not deserve to be upset.

'Yes, OK.' She hung up the telephone. When pigs fly, she thought, moving to lift the young boy from his chair and hugging him tightly to her; she nuzzled his neck while blinking a stray tear from her eye.

Gianfranco slipped the telephone into the inside pocket of his expertly tailored jacket, and strode across the concourse to the boarding gate for his flight. It was a new experience for him to have to persuade a woman to see him, and one he was not sure he liked. His hard mouth twisted in a wry grimace. He'd give it one more try. If Kelly turned up on Friday night, fine. If she didn't he was not pursuing her. His decision made, he handed his boarding pass to the female attendant with a broad smile, and quite unconsciously made the girl's day.

'Who was that on the telephone?' Judy asked as she walked into the kitchen, wearing only a blue satin robe.

'It was for me,' Kelly mumbled as she held Andrea in her arms.

'Ah, the boyfriend,' Judy said, and, moving to where Kelly stood, took Andrea from her. 'And this is my favourite boyfriend.' She kissed her son good morning, then placed him on his feet on the floor.

Kelly smiled; whatever Judy's faults, she did love her son.

'It's no good hanging around with a silly smile on your face, Kelly,' said Judy, totally misinterpreting the reason for the smile. 'Take my advice and drop the local boy. You are a good-looking woman—you should set your sights a whole lot higher. Go after someone like Count Maldini, a real catch. Last night I could see he was interested—yours was the only hand he kissed,' Judy opined with a sigh. 'But then, even if you got him, keeping him would be the problem.' Picking up a cup, she filled it with coffee from the pot and walked out with the comment, 'For Carlo, poor dear; he is feeling very sorry for himself this morning.'

Judy's comment gave Kelly pause for thought. She was intelligent, educated and considered herself as good as any other person on the planet. Gianfranco was a count. So what? Perhaps she had overreacted. He had called this morning, as promised. He did still want to see her and explain—well, according to him anyway. Surely he deserved a hearing, or was she the inverted snob he had intimated?

By the next morning Kelly had reached a decision: she would meet Gianfranco on Friday and hear what he had to say…

On Thursday afternoon Kelly was sitting on a plane winging its way back to England, glad to be going home and back to reality. On Tuesday Carlo Bertoni had declared there was no point staying in Italy any longer, since, as he could not compete in the yacht race, he might as well get back to work in London. Generously he had suggested Kelly stay on, on holiday, until the end of her contract in ten days' time. Marta was staying that long anyway, and Kelly had immediately accepted his offer.

But on Wednesday morning she had been leafing through the pages of the national newspaper and seen a picture of Count Maldini taken at a reception in New York on the Monday evening, with a stunning-looking redhead on his arm. Kelly had been able to fool herself no more; the affair, fling, was over, and there was no point in deluding herself otherwise. It was time she cut loose any connection whatsoever with Count Maldini.

On Thursday evening she said goodbye to the Bertoni family at Heathrow Airport. They were heading for their London townhouse and Kelly was heading for her family home: a small three-bedroom house in a quiet area of Bournemouth.

'Pregnant,' the doctor declared, and Kelly groaned. Her periods had always been irregular, and she had not been

sick or dizzy, or had any of the complaints usually connected with pregnancy. She had felt lousy in general, but
she had put that down to crying herself to sleep most nights
over Gianfranco. It had only been a month ago, when she'd
realised she could not fasten her jeans, that she'd been
brave enough to check dates. It was only what she had
feared for the last four weeks, but to hear Dr Jones confirm
it was still a shock.

'You really should have seen me a lot sooner, Kelly.
Still, no harm done, you're remarkably fit. I gather there is
no father on the horizon?' he prompted gently. He had
known the young girl before him all her life, he watched
her mother die in childbirth, and her father die of cancer,
and now this. 'By the date you gave me, you are thirteen
weeks pregnant.'

'Yes, that would be right. Thank you, Dr Jones.' Kelly
exited the surgery, clasping a card in her hand for her first
ante-natal appointment.

Sitting in the coffee shop of the largest department store
in Bournemouth, gazing dazedly at the Christmas decora-
tions, Kelly was sure things could not get worse. But they
did.

Judy Bertoni appeared out of nowhere. Apparently she
was visiting her parents for the day. Kelly cursed the fact
she had taken off her coat and hung it on the stand provided, and spent the next half-hour wondering how she
could leave without revealing when she stood up that she
had filled out somewhat. The jersey wool tube skirt and
matching sweater did nothing to disguise it. Eventually she
had no option but to get up, as one of the side-effects of
her pregnancy was a constant desire to visit the bathroom.

Eagle-eyed, figure-conscious Judy noticed immediately,
and Kelly was subjected to a long speech on the inadvis-
ability of dating a local Italian boy, and 'I told you so'.

Kelly was sorely tempted to blurt out who the father was, but managed to restrain herself. Judy, in her Mother Teresa act, promised she would keep in touch and send her Andrea's cast-offs. Kelly should have been grateful, but she wasn't; she felt sick and fat and fed-up.

She was even fatter and more fed-up when she returned from work at six on a cold Friday night in January. After a refreshing shower, and a meal of chicken and chips, she finally settled down on the sofa, prepared to spend the evening relaxing. With a Mozart tape in her Walkman, she held the earplugs to her stomach. She had read somewhere that music was good for the unborn baby and she hoped it was true.

The doorbell rang.

'Sugar!' she exclaimed, and, hauling herself up off the sofa, moved slowly to the door. It was probably Margaret. Since the house next door had been sold while Kelly had been in Italy, her new neighbour—a middle-aged spinster with an elderly mother who suffered from Alzheimer's and a bachelor brother, Jim, to look after—had taken to calling on Kelly. She hadn't the heart to turn the woman away.

'Just coming,' Kelly called as the doorbell rang again, longer and louder. 'Where's the fire?' she muttered under her breath, and opened the front door.

'Do you usually open the door without first enquiring who it is?' Gianfranco queried with a frown of grim disapproval creasing his broad brow.

In the first second of recognition her blue eyes widened, her heart leaping with joy, but instantly reality intruded. She'd tried to tell herself she was over him, had put him out of her mind and her heart. But seeing him before her, looking as rakishly handsome as ever, with a camel cashmere overcoat worn over a perfectly tailored dark business suit, his black hair rumpled by the winter wind, she knew she was not.

'What's it to you?' she snapped, angry at her own weakness where this man was concerned. At the same time she wished she were wearing something more glamorous.

Gianfranco's dark eyes swept over her face, taking in the tumbled mass of fine blonde hair, the slight blue shadows beneath her magnificent sapphire eyes, the beauty of her face not withstanding her belligerent expression. She did not look delighted to see him, and, lowering his gaze to where her breasts pressed firm against the soft blue wool of her sweater, and lower still to where the garment stretched over the soft mound of her stomach, he knew why. So it was true... He took a deep steadying breath.

'Your protection is everything to me—you are the mother of my baby,' Gianfranco declared firmly as he stepped into the hall and closed the door behind him.

What little colour she had drained from Kelly's face, and her blue eyes widened to their fullest extent as she gazed up in pure shock at the man towering over her. Gianfranco here, in her home, and he knew she was having his baby... 'But...how...?' She swayed, suddenly feeling faint, and could not get the sentence out, a host of different emotions tangling her tongue.

'Come, let's sit down.' Gianfranco grabbed her arm. 'It can't be good for you standing in a cold hall in your condition.' He unerringly led her into the sitting room of her own home.

'Now wait a minute,' she finally managed, shakily finding her voice.

'I think we have waited rather too many minutes—months, in fact,' he teased, his dark eyes roaming pointedly down to her stomach and back to her face as he led her to the sofa and eased her down into it, lowering his long length beside her and taking her hand in one of his.

The closeness of his large male body, the familiar male scent that was uniquely Gianfranco, all conspired to make her heart race. A dull red flush suffused her cheeks. It wasn't fair; he only had to touch her and, even fat and pregnant, she still felt the same instant sensual response, every hair on her body standing on end.

'How did you find me—and how did you know I was pregnant?' Kelly asked the question she should have asked the minute he walked in the door, looking somewhere over his left shoulder, unwilling to meet his knowing brown eyes. The fact he had accepted the baby she was carrying was his, without her having to say a word, had totally stunned her.

Gianfranco was not the sort of man to do anything without a reason, and she could think of no valid reason for his being here. He had made his opinion of unwanted pregnancy abundantly clear the one time they had made love. In her secret dreams she had sometimes thought of him turning up on her doorstep and declaring his undying love. But harsh reality told her he was much more likely to take one look at her, perhaps give her a cheque and definitely run.

'I was at a New Year's Eve party in Rome. Judy Bertoni was there and naturally I asked after you. She took great delight in telling me you had succumbed to the charms of some local man in Desenzano and that you are pregnant,' he told her simply. He saw no need to elaborate on the bare facts.

'You didn't tell her it was you?' Kelly asked hastily. The fewer people who knew what an idiot she had been the better, was her reasoning.

One dark brow arched sardonically. 'I am not a complete

fool, Kelly, I knew I had to check with you first. But it took all my considerable will-power not to ask her for your address,' Gianfranco said with a grim smile. 'Instead I hired a private detective to discover where you lived.' He gave a very Latin shrug of his shoulders. 'And here I am.' He squeezed her hand in his.

Kelly's blue eyes involuntarily followed the movement of his broad shoulders, and swallowed hard. He really was a magnificent male animal, and very much here... Not for her, she tried to tell herself, but her raging hormones thought otherwise.

'You tracked me down?' She latched on to the detective bit, amazed at the nerve of the man. 'Do you do that with all your dates?' she demanded curtly, not sure she liked the idea but helplessly flustered by the sensual warmth of his hand holding hers. Was it only she who felt the electric tension in the air? she wondered, chewing nervously on her bottom lip. Though, on second thoughts, she couldn't help feeling flattered that he had hired a detective to find her, but she was also wary—she didn't trust him an inch.

'So why are you here?' she demanded bravely, tilting her head to look up at him, and the gleam of triumph in his dark eyes sent a shiver down her spine. Suddenly she had a horrible suspicion she knew the answer to her own question, and she immediately voiced her fear. 'If you think I am going to have an abortion, forget it!' she declared, her blue eyes flashing flames. 'This is my child, my responsibility, and you can get lost.'

'*Dio!* Jumping to conclusions as usual.' Gianfranco leapt to his feet and stormed across the small living room. Tearing off his topcoat, he flung it on a chair and flipped open his jacket; he was boiling with rage. He had been ever since, after months of fighting his desire for Kelly, he had succumbed to the temptation to seek out Judy Bertoni and ask after her. With relish Judy had told him Kelly was pregnant by some local Italian youth. Of course, he had known immediately he was the father, and when he had got over the initial shock he had been furious that Kelly had not told him herself.

'How dare you say that to me?' he demanded arrogantly. She saw the naked anger flare in his eyes, and something more she did not recognise. 'To suggest I would wish to kill my own child? What kind of monster do you take me for? What did I ever do to you to give you such a low opinion of me?'

'Pretend to be someone else,' Kelly slipped in snidely.

He stilled in the middle of the floor, his broad shoulders tensing, and said, 'So I am to pay for that one silly mistake for the rest of my life. Is that why you never saw fit to inform me you were having my child?' he asked hardly, his hooded eyes half-closed, masking his expression. 'Is that why you never turned up for our date on the Friday evening?' With each question he moved a step closer. 'Is that why you now accuse me of wanting to murder my child?' Gianfranco asked bitterly, his dark eyes flaring with contempt. 'Pay-back time on your part? My God, I thought better of you than that, Kelly.'

'You actually kept our date?' She was staggered by his revelation, her brief burst of anger draining away as she accepted the thought; it pleased her enormously, and restored some of her battered pride. She had spent the last few months in abject misery because of this man. At the lowest point, when her pregnancy had been confirmed, she had been tempted to call him, but she only had to recall his horror the one time they had made love and he'd discovered she was not protected to know it would be a waste of time. But he was obviously not the complete bastard she had thought him.

Gianfranco focused on her seated figure with a blistering fury that seemed to increase with each word he spoke. 'Kept it? I waited all night and drank myself into oblivion. And where were you? Marta the housekeeper told me the next day. Back home in England after refusing a free holiday. That's how much you cared.'

As the meaning of his outburst hit her Kelly could only stare at him open-mouthed. He actually had cared about her. The notion was as startling as it was seductive.

'Nothing to say? I am not surprised,' Gianfranco drawled with savage derision. 'You used me, got yourself pregnant and came scurrying back to England without the least intention of ever telling me.'

'No. It wasn't like that,' Kelly burst out impulsively. 'I was going to meet you on the Friday, but...' She trailed off, nervously moistening her dry lips with the tip of her tongue.

Gianfranco's black brows arched in surprise. The Kelly he remembered had been bluntly honest, to the point of indiscretion. He drew a steadying breath, banking down his anger, and his eyes narrowing on her lovely face, he took a step towards her. 'But what, Kelly...?' he prompted silkily, and in another stride he had crossed the space dividing them and settled on the sofa next to her. He reached out and caught her by the shoulders, gently urged her back against the soft cushions. 'Tell me...' Anger would get him nowhere with Kelly, she had too much spirit, but a little judicious questioning should do the trick.

Gianfranco's brilliant eyes clashed with hers and her breath caught in her throat, his proximity doing unimaginable things to her nervous system. 'I...I...' Kelly stammered to a halt, embarrassed by what she had almost revealed.

'Go on,' he encouraged, his dark eyes burning into hers with mesmerising effect.

Why not tell him? She was no good at dissembling anyway. 'On the Wednesday I saw a picture of you and your latest girlfriend—a very beautiful redhead—taken two nights before in New York, in the newspaper,' she confessed bluntly. 'There did not seem much point after that.'

Her response stunned him. He drew back slightly, and looked down at her with incredulous eyes for a long moment. 'You were jealous…' he declared, and for the first time in months his firm lips parted over gleaming white teeth in a broad self-satisfied smile.

'I was not,' she denied adamantly, but the scarlet blush that enveloped her face told its own story.

Gianfranco's hand slipped from her shoulder to encircle her waist and pull her towards him, his night-dark eyes never leaving hers for a second. 'No matter,' he murmured in a low-pitched undertone, and covered her lips with his own in a long, slow, sensual kiss that drove every sensible thought from Kelly's mind, and ignited the familiar electrifying sensations in every part of her body.

Dazed and breathless when he finally lifted his head, she could only stare at him in bemusement. 'Why did you do that?' she murmured.

Gianfranco eased her back against the cushions, lifted a large hand, and rested the tip of a finger against the pulse beating madly in her throat. 'To prove you still want me,' he drawled huskily. 'An essential prerequisite in a wife.' Cupping her chin, he added, 'And we are going to be married, Kelly.'

On seeking out Kelly, Gianfranco had told himself he simply wanted to check up on her and make sure she was financially provided for. He was as surprised as Kelly looked to hear the offer of marriage come out of his mouth.

But the more he thought about it, the more sense it made. His mother would be delighted—she was always nagging him to marry, and produce an heir. With Kelly already pregnant there could be no doubt of the girl's fertility, unlike poor Olivia. Yes, it was the right decision.

Kelly stared at him blankly, unable to believe her ears, and, leaning over her, his breath fanning her cheek, he slipped a hand under her legs and suddenly she was stretched out on the sofa.

'Wait.' She tried to object, but the word 'marriage' had shocked her rigid.

Gianfranco lifted his head, a wide, confident smile parting his lips. 'We have both waited long enough, Kelly.' And then he kissed her again.

She wanted to resist, and she did try—she lifted her hands to his chest to push him away, but feeling the firm beat of his heart beneath her fingertips had the opposite effect, and of their own volition her hands snaked up to clasp around his neck. Her lips parted, her tongue duelling with his instinctively in a desperate hunger of passion too long denied.

His hand slipped under her sweater to curve over the full mound of her breast, and she quivered, heat surging through her veins. Pressed against the awesome male body, she forgot everything but the feel, the scent of him. She ached for him.

Gianfranco groaned, raised his head, and with one deft movement pushed her jumper up so her lush, unfettered breasts were open to his gaze. 'Dio, I love your breasts.' Black eyes glittering, he ran an exploring finger over the pouting rosy tips, and her whole body arched in shivering delight. His dark head lowered and his mouth closed over a rigid peak.

'Gianfranco.' Kelly moaned his name in a pleasure that was almost pain.

His head jerked up, eyes clashing with hers. 'Did I hurt you? The baby, is it safe?'

CHAPTER FIVE

THE baby! It was like a douche of cold water on her over-heated flesh. Struggling to sit up, she pushed at his mighty chest. 'Get off me.'

Gianfranco reared back and, lifting her into a sitting position, smoothed her sweater down over her breasts. 'I promised myself I would not jump on you, Kelly, but I only have to look at you to want you,' he said huskily. 'Even with this glorious bump.' One large hand spread out over her stomach, and right at that moment the baby kicked. 'It moved,' he declared, his dark eyes fixed on her stomach in rapt fascination. 'I can't wait till we are married and I can look after you both properly.' He lifted his head. 'I didn't hurt you or the baby?' His gleaming eyes sought hers for reassurance.

'No, no, you didn't,' Kelly said stiltedly. She could not lie to him, but neither was she going to let him walk all over her. It was the sheer conceit of the man that angered Kelly. She hadn't seen him for almost five months, and he strolled back into her life and offered marriage as if he was doing her a favour. 'As for marriage—that will not be necessary,' she told him bluntly.

He did not want her; it was only the child he was interested in. And, getting to her feet, she glanced down at where he sat, the look of puzzled outrage in his dark eyes enough to make her want to laugh. 'I can do without your noble gesture—I am perfectly capable of looking after my own child,' she said sweetly. 'Now, would you like a coffee before you leave?' she offered.

Before she could move, Gianfranco leapt to his feet, his hands grasping her shoulders.

'What the hell are you talking about, Kelly? Noble? I am not noble—I haven't a noble bone in my body.'

'I thought all ''counts'' were noblemen, or supposed to be,' she prompted mockingly.

He paused, his hard mouth curving in a bitter, cynical smile. 'So that is what is bothering you—the fact I have a title. I should have guessed you would be the opposite of most women of my acquaintance, who love the idea.' His hands tightened on her shoulders, his brown eyes clashing with her blue ones, and her heart gave a curious lurch at the glittering intensity of his gaze.

'I never wanted nor ever expected to have a title—that was my brother's birthright. But three years ago he was killed in a yachting accident and the title was thrust upon me. Do you really think I enjoyed giving up my freewheeling lifestyle working in the financial markets of the world to take on the burden of the family estates as well, to have to work twice as hard with twice as much responsibility?' he spelt out grimly. 'The day I met you was the first time in three years I had taken a weekend off, and the first time I had been back to Desenzano since my brother's death.'

'Why are you telling me all this now?' she asked, intensely aware of his hard male body towering over her, his long fingers kneading her slender shoulders, as if he would force her to listen.

'Because the minute I saw you, so beautiful, so carefree, I decided to forget about everything and give myself a holiday and try to get to know you. So, yes, you are right in a way, I should have told you who I was, but for once I simply wanted to enjoy myself; is that so hard to understand?'

Kelly had never coveted wealth. She enjoyed her life,

and as long as she had enough to get by on she was quite happy, but she could understand great wealth must bring with it great responsibilities. 'Yes, I suppose so.' The thought that he thought she was beautiful was balm to her bruised heart, and slowly she was recovering from the shock of seeing him again. 'But marriage?' That was something else again, she thought, unaware she had voiced that thought out loud.

'Yes, Kelly,' Gianfranco cut in, pulling her closer to the hard heat of his body. 'You will marry me, and have my child. I have not spent the last few months going crazy over a blonde-haired little spitfire to be turned down now.'

He smoothed a possessive hand over her quivering length, lingering on her stomach. 'You are mine, and this baby is mine,' he husked quietly, and smiled.

How did he do that? One minute he was all outraged predatory male and moments later he was smiling tenderly into her guarded blue eyes. 'Yes,' she murmured, thinking, in her confused state, he was asking if the baby was his.

His dark head lowered and he let his tongue trace the fullness of her lips before delving into the moist depths. His hand slid down her back to the base of her spine, moving against her in a way that made her blatantly aware of his arousal.

Kelly tried to remain rigid in his embrace, but her body softened against the hard heat of Gianfranco's massive frame.

'You want me, and I want you; what more is there to say?' He breathed the words against her mouth and softly to her throat and ear, then back once more to her pouting lips. He nudged her lips apart again and dipped into her mouth with his tongue, in a rhythm that made a moan rise in her throat.

'Gianni,' she gasped helplessly, but she retained enough

common sense to know he was deliberately trying to seduce her.

He felt her tremble and loved her reaction. 'You called me Gianni; you have not forgotten.' He groaned with feeling against her mouth, scanning her with glittering eyes filled with hunger and something more. He stared down into her dazed yet wary eyes and he wanted to take her there and then, his body screaming for release. Instead he drew in a steadying breath and eased her to arm's length. 'Perhaps a drink is in order, but not coffee—I need something stronger,' he opined bluntly.

Kelly heard the faint humour in his tone and smiled. He sounded like a man sorely tried. 'I think I can oblige. There is half a bottle of whisky left over from Christmas in the kitchen. Have a seat and I'll get it.'

She badly needed to put some space between them. He was right about her wanting him. She did, always had since the first moment she'd set eyes on him. Gianni or Gianfranco, it didn't matter; he was the man she loved, she acknowledged as she walked into the kitchen on shaking legs. If she was honest with herself, Gianfranco's surprising offer of marriage was more than she had ever hoped for, and it was very tempting. She opened a cupboard and withdrew the bottle of amber nectar.

A few minutes later she walked back into the living room, with a tray bearing a glass of whisky and a glass of milk. A quick glance and she saw Gianfranco was leaning against the mantelpiece, one hand fingering the silver-framed photograph of a couple with their arms around each other. His eyes caught hers before she could look away. 'Your parents?' He indicated the picture. 'I never thought to ask…where are they?'

'Both dead,' she said softly.

'So you are alone in the world,' he declared grimly. In

one lithe stride he was beside her, and, taking the tray from her hands, he placed it on the coffee table. Straightening up, he handed her the glass of milk. 'You should not carry anything in your condition.'

His fingers brushed hers as she took the glass, sending a tingling sensation up her arm. Their eyes met, his dark and knowing, hers guarded. 'I'm not ill, only pregnant,' she said drily. 'I'm still at work,' she tagged on, sinking down into a convenient armchair with a sigh. She was also tired and emotionally confused, but she had no intention of telling Gianfranco. Instead she lifted the glass to her mouth and took a long swallow of the cool creamy liquid.

'You still work!' he exclaimed, and stared at her as if she had gone mad. 'That's it.' Gianfranco drained his glass of whisky in one gulp, banged it down on the table, and turned to frown down at her. He had flown to England angry, not sure what he was going to do about Kelly, but one look at her and he had heard himself asking her to marry him. Thank God he had. It appalled him to realise she was alone in the world, and it also brought home to him how little he really knew about her. Well, all that had to change, he decided in his usual arrogant manner.

'As I remember, you were going to work as a research chemist.' His dark brows drew together in a thunderous frown. 'That is out. There is no way you should be anywhere near a laboratory—you could catch anything, do untold damage to our child.'

Her head tilted back, her blue eyes lifting to his, and what she saw made her suck in her breath—he was deadly serious. 'But...'

'No buts. You will resign tomorrow—in fact, I will do it for you.'

'Now wait just a minute...'

'No. On this I will not budge. As my wife, you are not working in a laboratory.'

'Gianfranco, really, it is the twenty-first century— women work all through their pregnancy at all sorts of jobs. Some go back three months after the child is born.'

'Not you,' he declared adamantly.

She could argue, she reasoned, but somehow she didn't want to. There was something very seductive about having a man take charge.

'You are not going to argue?' One dark brow arched in puzzlement as she watched and she almost giggled. He was standing over her, his great body taut with tension.

'Do you want me to?' she asked softly. Incredible as it seemed, she was beginning to think that perhaps there was some hope for them. She loved him, she was carrying his child, and he wanted to marry her. Common sense told her at least to listen.

'No. Oh, no. Kelly.' To her astonishment, he dropped to his knees at her feet.

He caught her hand and turned it over in his much larger one. 'I know our relationship got off to a rocky start,' he said, picking his words with care. 'I know this is not the ideal situation to find ourselves in. But know this, Kelly.' His rough, deep voice was thick with some overwhelming emotion. 'I really do want to marry you, child or no child, the sooner the better.'

Kelly trembled as Gianfranco lifted her hand to his lips and pressed a tender kiss into her palm, before raising his head, his gaze roaming over her beautiful face. There was no mistaking the sincerity, the simmering passion in the deep brown eyes that finally met hers.

'Kelly, my love, give me a second chance.' He took a deep, rasping breath. 'I don't want to rush you into anything you don't want, but marry me soon,' he pleaded huskily. 'You know it makes sense.'

Kelly wasn't aware she was giving him a second chance, she thought muzzily, but, as his arms drifted around her again and pulled her gently into the warmth of his embrace, she didn't resist. She could not. His dark head lowered and his lips found hers. This was where the last hour had been leading; this was what she had been afraid of. She was incapable of controlling her own response. Why deny it, she asked herself with a flash of insight, when she wanted him so much? Her senses were swimming with pleasure, her mouth clinging to his as he held her tightly against him, his tongue darting between her lips, exploring her mouth with an urgent passion.

'*Dio*, you feel so good. You don't know what you do to me, *cara*.' His deep voice shook as he eased her slightly away from him. 'Say yes, Kelly.'

For months she had been telling herself she would be fine as a single parent. But was she being fair to her unborn child? Kelly asked herself, studying Gianfranco's handsome face with brilliant blue eyes. Now she had a choice; he was offering marriage, and two parents must be better than one. It was no contest because, dear heaven, she loved him.

Instead of the 'yes' that trembled on her lips Kelly heard herself ask, 'Who was the redhead?'

'Natalie. The wife of an American cousin of mine. Her husband was in the Far East on business and I deputised for him at the charity dinner,' he explained huskily. 'Only at the dinner, I swear.'

For a long moment she stared into his incredible eyes, and she believed him. 'In that case...' She reached her arms around his neck, urging him back to her, 'Yes, oh, yes.' Her long lashes fluttered down over her brilliant blue eyes, her fingers tangling in the silky black hair of his head, her lips blindly seeking his again.

She never saw the flare of triumph in his night-dark eyes as he gathered her close and kissed her long and slow, and when she finally opened her eyes she gazed up at him, totally enslaved all over again.

'You have made me the happiest man alive.'

'Happiest man...' she murmured, floating in a sensuous bubble. 'Are you sure you want to marry me?' She had to ask. It was like a dream, and she wanted to pinch herself to make sure it was true.

'I have never wanted anything more in my life, except perhaps tonight I want to make love to you, as I should have done the first time. Long and slow, very slow.'

'Sounds good,' she sighed, and tightened her hands behind his head.

'No, not here—the bedroom.' And, lifting her in his arms, he carried her out of the room, up the stairs, and without hesitation walked into the first bedroom he came to. One glance at the double bed and Gianfranco wanted to lay her down on it. But he forced himself to lower Kelly slowly to her feet.

As if waking from a dream, Kelly stood in the middle of the floor and looked up. Gianfranco was towering over her, his arms linked loosely around her waist. His eyes, dark with desire, roamed over her small frame, but when his hands reached for the bottom of her sweater she froze.

Suddenly she was terribly conscious of her altered physical state. 'No,' Kelly whispered and grasped his hands with hers. 'I'm not the same.' She looked up into his handsome face and placed a restraining hand on his chest. 'I'm fat— my waist has gone,' she said, scarlet with embarrassment.

Gianfranco wanted to laugh, she looked so beautiful, so woebegone, but he had more sense than to do so. 'You are not fat, Kelly, you are luscious and swollen with my child. I have never seen you more beautiful.' And, lifting her hand from his chest, he led her to the bed. Then, squeezing her hand, he added, 'But if you are nervous you can undress me first.' His dark eyes held hers as he quickly removed his shoes and socks, and then, straightening, more slowly removed his tie, undid the first two buttons of his shirt. 'Help me, Kelly,' he husked.

Intrigued, she forgot her own embarrassment and, sliding her small hands over his chest, she quickly unbuttoned the rest of his shirt. He slipped it from his shoulders and Kelly slid her hands back up over the tanned hair-roughened chest with tactile delight. 'You feel hot,' Kelly murmured, lifting fascinated eyes to his. 'And so hard.'

Gianfranco almost groaned out loud. She had got that right; he was so hard he thought he'd burst. But even if it killed him he was going to make it right for her this time, he vowed. He smiled gently. 'Now the trousers,' he prompted.

Her head dipped, her slender fingers making short work of the waist fastening, but she hesitated a second before pulling down the zip, her knuckles stroking the rigid length of him through the fine fabric of his shorts.

There was something very exciting, empowering, about undressing a man, Kelly thought, her heart racing as she gently eased his trousers down over his hips, then, dropping to her knees, she slid them down his long legs. Intent upon her task, she never saw the grimace of agony on his face as her long hair brushed against his naked thighs and the hard length of his arousal, barely covered by black silk.

Stooping, Gianfranco lifted her to her feet. 'Enough,' he said huskily as he bent to her mouth. 'I can't wait much longer.'

As his mouth covered hers his hand slipped under her

sweater and lifted it, his hands gliding up over her breasts, caressing her with expert tenderness.

Kelly shivered, her whole body flushing with heat, and lifted her arms, but before she could put them around him he had whipped her jumper over her head, and claimed her mouth once more.

She forgot about her thickened waistline, forgot everything, and mindlessly kissed him back.

He lifted his head and pulled her arms from around him. Stepping back, he whipped off his shorts and slid his hands down the elastic waist of her leggings, easing them down her hips.

'No panties, Kelly?' He grinned, but his eyes darkened to black as he looked at her. 'I didn't know how beautiful a woman could be until now,' he husked softly, blatantly scrutinising her high firm breasts with their rosy tips so hard, so tempting, the soft swell of her stomach, and lower to the long shapely legs and the cluster of pale curls at the apex of her thighs.

'Kelly, you are the most utterly feminine woman I have ever seen,' he declared, his breathing heavy. He lifted a finger and slowly stroked over the smooth skin of her shoulder, then lower in a line across the soft curve of her breasts.

Helplessly she swayed towards him, her own eyes raking over his bronzed torso, the symmetry of muscle and sinew, the savage splendour of his powerful aroused body. She murmured his name and reached out to touch him, with a look in her sapphire eyes as old as Eve.

He groaned with sheer impatience and lifted her in his arms again, sinking to the bed with her.

The full contact of his naked body with hers made Kelly dizzy with desire. The blood drummed in her ears, and blindly she reached for him. Gianfranco reared up over her, filling her vision, and bent his head to her breast.

She felt the warm, moist pressure of his mouth taking the rigid tip inside and she moaned softly, her body arching towards the sensual pleasure of his mouth. Her hands clung to his wide shoulders, her fingers digging into his flesh, helpless captive to the erotic expertise of his tongue and teeth.

His hand moved to tenderly caress the soft mound of her belly, and all the while his mouth and other hand teased her breasts, his thumb scraping over the rigid tip, driving her crazy, her body writhing in an explicit demand for more. 'Gianfranco,' she pleaded.

He lifted his head, his black eyes glittering with passion. 'Slowly, slowly,' he rasped, and lowered his head to brush her lips with his.

Kelly eagerly opened her mouth for him as he eased his hand from her stomach down to the soft curls guarding her feminine core, making her body tremble. His fingers delved into the soft velvet folds to find the moist heat, and stroked and touched until she groaned out loud.

He lifted his head to look into her passion-glazed eyes. 'You want me,' he breathed. 'And I want you.'

Kelly bit into the flesh of his chest, wild with need; she didn't understand the urge, but her mouth found a small male nipple and licked and kissed it, her nails digging into his flesh harder and harder as his long fingers continued to mercilessly explore her body. Her heart hammered and she writhed against him. She felt him shudder and groan, and, made brave by the passion riding her, slid a hand down to his powerful body until she reached the rigid length of him and closed around him.

'No,' Gianfranco rasped, and, catching her hand, he pulled it from his body. 'Not yet; I don't want to hurt you.'

And, rolling onto his back, he lifted her over him, his night-black eyes dilated with passion. 'Trust me,' he grated as he slowly surged up into the sweet, hot heart of her femininity.

Her brilliant sapphire eyes widened, the pupils expanding until they almost eclipsed the blue. A whimper of sound escaped her throat as he drew her towards him, his mouth lifting to capture a taut nipple. He suckled her tender flesh with an avid enjoyment that drove her wild with desire as his strong hands held her waist, keeping her exactly where he wanted her. Her head fell back, her hands flat on his broad chest, fingers digging into his flesh as slowly, with subtle movements of his hands and hips, he rocked her higher and higher until she was drowning in the unimaginable wonder of pure sensation. He was hard and hot, and drove her to the edge of ecstasy—more pleasure than she had ever imagined existed. Her nails scratched across his chest and she cried out his name, as he swiftly reversed their positions. For a second he stared down at her, hunger and determination warring in the dark, taut features.

'This time, Kelly, this time for you,' he said hoarsely, and then moved again.

He filled her completely, and Kelly was lost in an all-encompassing passion, a primeval need, that drove her mindlessly onto another plane where time was suspended and her shuddering body reached and found the little death, the pitch of human passion, in a fierce, convulsive climax. Her blue eyes flew wide open in shocked wonder at the awesome joy of fulfilment. His harsh groan of satisfaction as he spilled his seed inside her mingled with her keening cry of his name.

Her hands clung to his broad shoulders, then softly stroked the sweat-damp skin. 'I thought the first time was wonderful, but…' She breathed unevenly, looking up into his night-black eyes.

'Shhh.' Gianfranco slipped onto his side. 'I know.' And, pressing soft little kisses to her face and hair, he held her tenderly against him.

'I never knew...' she whispered, breaking the silence, rubbing her head against a strong tanned shoulder like a satisfied kitten.

Gianfranco looked into her dazed blue eyes. 'Now you know why I was so angry the first time,' he said huskily, with all the confidence of a man who knew he had satisfied his lady.

Tension snaked through her. Sadly she remembered the aftermath last time. 'Because I might get pregnant,' she muttered with a slight frown. 'But that hardly applies now.'

With a deep throaty chuckle, Gianfranco planted a swift kiss on her small nose. 'No, my sweet. It wasn't so much the fact you were innocent that made me angry, but because, though I was loath to admit it, I never gave you the satisfaction you should have had,' he declared ruefully. 'I lost control. You were too innocent to know the difference, but I did. It was quite a blow to my male ego, so I took it out on you, and for that I apologise.'

'Oh, oh, I see.' A dawning realisation lit her wide blue eyes as they met his. Gianfranco, her macho lover, feeling vulnerable as the next man about his performance in bed? The thought made her grin.

'It wasn't funny at the time.' He nipped teasingly at the small lobe of her ear. 'And I promise you it will never happen again. I am going to spend the rest of my life making love to you to prove it.' He found her lips and kissed her long and lingeringly, then trailed kisses in an erotic path down her throat, her breasts, and to the soft swell of her stomach.

Kelly glanced down to where his dark head lay against her stomach and she wanted to believe a miracle had happened and he loved her. 'You don't have to marry me,' she murmured reluctantly, not wanting to burst the miraculous bubble she seemed to be floating in, but knowing she had to give him the choice.

Gianfranco rubbed his cheek against her belly, and, caressing the smooth mound, he pressed worshipful kisses on her silken skin. 'Our son,' he said, and, rearing up on one elbow, he let his other large hand gently, almost reverently, massage her stomach. 'And I do have to marry you, because I never want to be apart from you again.'

Kelly looked long and hard into his dark eyes, wanting to believe him. But was it her or a son he wanted? she asked herself. 'It might be a girl.'

'Girl, boy. I don't care as long as I have you.' Then he started to make love to her again, with a gentle seductive tenderness, an expertise that banished all her fears, and finally convinced her he loved her as he completely overwhelmed her all over again.

CHAPTER SIX

THEY were married four days later on the Friday, and Kelly, walking out of the registrar's office with Gianfranco's arm around her shoulders, was still reeling from the speed of it all.

'Wait.' Margaret, who had agreed with her brother Jim to be their witness, stopped them on the steps. 'You have to have a photograph,' she said, and raised her camera to her eye. 'Say cheese.'

'I'd rather say sex,' Gianfranco whispered in Kelly's ear, and brought a beaming smile to her face.

'You are insatiable,' Kelly chuckled a moment later, her blue eyes laughing up at him. The past few days they had made love morning, noon and night. In between, Gianfranco had organised everything. Kelly had resigned from her job, and her family home was up for sale with a local estate agent, Gianfranco insisting her home was going to be with him from now on.

The only thing Kelly had done herself was shop; she had bought a trousseau of sorts, given the limitations of her figure: lacy underwear and a couple of satin nightgowns, a few smart-casual clothes and one cocktail dress, plus the outfit she was wearing.

It was a winter-white cashmere dress, long-sleeved, with a softly curved bow-neck that revealed a hint of cleavage. The fine wool skimmed her figure, and flared ever so slightly from her knees almost to her feet. Elegant and ideal for a January day, it moulded her stomach, but Kelly didn't mind. If famous film stars could reveal their bumps in the nude, she told herself, her small tummy was perfectly acceptable. Apart from her posy of yellow rosebuds, her only adornment was the diamond crucifix around her slender throat.

'You look beautiful,' Gianfranco told her as he helped her into the waiting car. 'My wife,' and he kissed her with a very self-satisfied grin on his handsome face.

Seated in the VIP lounge at the airport, Kelly glanced across at her very new husband. He was standing by the business desk, sending messages to heaven knew where, while they waited for their flight to be called for Rome. He made her heart leap with love. He looked so devastatingly handsome in a perfectly tailored dark navy three-piece suit, and brilliant white silk shirt. A lock of black hair fell forward over his broad brow, and she watched with some amusement as he gesticulated with one hand while talking on the telephone. In that moment it hit her how very Latin he was.

The briefest of frowns marred her smooth brow as for the first time she wondered how she would get on living in what was for her a foreign country, with Gianfranco and his family.

Kelly stood on the balcony later that day and gaped in awe at the view before her. The whole of Rome appeared spread out below. Two strong arms wrapped around her non-existent waist, and a dark head bent and a warm mouth nuzzled her ear. 'You like the view, *cara*?'

Like it? She loved it! She'd unpacked her suitcase while Gianfranco had made a few urgent business calls, then he'd given her a swift tour of the penthouse—the sitting room was comfortable but elegant, decorated in blue and gold, the furniture was a selection of tasteful antiques, while the master bedroom was a symphony in cream and dark rose and the other three bedrooms were just as elegant.

She turned slowly in the arms that held her, and beamed up into Gianfranco's darkly handsome face. 'The view is magnificent—the apartment is magnificent.' Reaching a slender finger to his face, she added, 'And you are magnificent.' As she traced the outline of his sensuous lips with the pad of one finger, her blue eyes meshed with his. 'Can we stay here forever?'

A long kiss later Gianfranco answered. 'Not for ever, but for the next three days certainly. Then we must go to my country estate, and I will have to get back to work.'

'Do you think your family will like me?' Kelly voiced her fear. 'Maybe you should have asked them to the wedding?' Gianfranco bent his head, his lips brushing hers again, and she savoured the sweetness with the tip of her tongue as he grinned down into her luminous blue eyes.

'They will love you, and there wasn't time to ask them to the wedding. Anyway, you have already met Mother and Olivia, and they know why we married. Mother is arranging a reception for you in two weeks' time to introduce you to everyone.' Something about what he said disturbed her, but before she had time to think he added, 'But right now I want to start the honeymoon.' Bending down, he scooped her bodily into his arms, with an easy strength that made her lace her arms around his neck and nuzzle her lips against the pulse that beat in the strong column of his throat as he carried her through to the bedroom.

'Do you have any idea how much I want you?' Gianfranco asked roughly as he lowered her to her feet and speedily divested her of her clothes. 'How much I ache for you?' And his own clothes were removed.

Kelly's heart raced at the sight of him. He was all-powerful, virile male, and the very air in the room seemed charged with an electric current of sensualism.

Gianfranco's dark eyes roamed possessively over her naked form, the high, firm breasts, then lower to the growing swell of her stomach, and lower still to the soft curve of her hips and thighs.

Kelly proudly exulted in his scrutiny; this was her husband. Her own gaze swept over his wide shoulders, the mat of soft, dark hair on his broad chest descending in a fine line to brush out and cradle his sex. She heard the harsh intake of his breath and the sudden rise and fall of his chest, and tilted back her head to look up at him.

Gianfranco's deep, dark eyes seemed to pierce her soul as he reached for her. 'Kelly, my wife,' he growled. 'At last.' He hauled her to him with a savage urgency that surprised her.

Her hands found his shoulders as his tongue plundered the tender interior of her mouth. He kissed her deep and long, his hard body burning against her, until her head swam and she could hardly breathe. Then he lifted her to the bed.

'Gianfranco.' Kelly surfaced long enough from the heady magic of his kiss to say his name.

'Who else?' he growled sexily. 'You are mine now.' He muttered something huskily in Italian before his mouth dipped down to capture one taut nipple and suckle her tender flesh with intense erotic delight that drove her wild with wanting.

In the long passion-filled hours that followed they fed off each other's hunger to the point of exhaustion. Kelly thought Gianfranco had taught her all about love in the past few days, but he still surprised her.

'You make me insatiable,' Gianfranco rasped on a shuddering sigh as he reluctantly withdrew from the sleek heart of her and drew her gently into the hard curve of his body. 'I must remember you are pregnant, and control myself.'

Kelly smiled. She had lost count of the times he had driven them both to the brink and over. 'A bit late now, my love,' she murmured sleepily, resting her head on the side of his chest, her long lashes falling down over her sapphire eyes. 'But it is our wedding night.' She whispered the words against his sweat-slicked skin, her body sated and exhausted.

A sound jerked her out of a deep sleep and, rolling over on the bed, she reached for Gianfranco and found only space. Hauling herself up into a sitting position, she blinked and looked around. Their holiday was obviously over.

The past three days had been the most marvellous of her life. Gianfranco had shown her Rome, the Colisseum, the Trevi fountain, where she'd thrown the obligatory coin, all the obvious tourist attractions, and a few not so obvious. There was the tiny church tucked away in a narrow street, with an altar screen of unbelievable beauty. A small restaurant with plastic tablecloths, serving the most mouthwatering food in Italy, according to her husband.

A sigh of sheer contentment was followed by her stomach's rumbling. She was eating for two and they had missed dinner again last night. Slipping out of bed, she padded to the bathroom and after a brisk shower she walked back into the bedroom, wearing only a large fluffy towel tucked around her body toga-style.

'Good morning, *cara*,' Gianfranco drawled huskily, placing a loaded tray containing coffee and a selection of pastries down on the bedside table. He walked towards her, his eyes bright with amusement at her scantily covered, rumpled state. 'Sorry to rush you, but I want to make it home by midday if possible.' He pressed a swift kiss on her lush lips.

'Monday morning and the honeymoon is over.' Kelly sighed dramatically, her blue eyes sparkling up at him; he looked devastatingly attractive in blue jeans and a black Armani sweater.

'Don't worry,' Gianfranco instructed, 'I will take you on a proper honeymoon—anywhere you want. The Maldives, the Caribbean. Once our child is born and we can be alone.' His deep voice dropped sexily and, lifting his hand, he brushed her hair behind one ear. The touch of his warm fingers and the sensual promise in his dark eyes made her heart skip a beat. 'I promise,' he mouthed against her slightly parted lips, and kissed her again. 'Now eat and pack and dress.' With a tender pat to her stomach, he spun on his heel and left the room.

Refreshed by the coffee and food, in five minutes she was dressed in a pair of pale grey trousers, in fine wool blend, and a crew-neck blue sweater. On her feet she wore comfortable black loafers, and she had draped a dove-grey leather jacket over the suitcase. She gave her hair a quick brush, leaving it to fall long and straight from a centre parting, and she was ready.

'Ready?' Gianfranco demanded sauntering back into the room and looping a long arm around her waist.

'I guess so.' Kelly's eyes were nervous as she glanced up at him. 'I hope your mother likes me...'

'You worry too much,' he teased, and kissed her again, and when she was suitably breathless he lifted his head. 'I adore you, and my mother likes whoever I like,' he drawled with unconscious arrogance, and, bending, he picked up the suitcase. 'Come on.'

If he thought he was reassuring Kelly he was wrong. Common sense told her no woman was going to be delighted to have missed her only son's wedding and then have him turn up with a pregnant wife. Acceptance was the best she could hope for, she reasoned, and the first seed of doubt took root in her heart. Had she done the right thing in marrying Gianfranco? She loved him, but would love be enough?

Kelly looked out of the window of the Ferrari with some trepidation as Gianfranco brought the car to a halt in a huge paved courtyard outside the impressive entrance portico of his family home. They had stopped on the way for lunch, but now they had arrived there was no ducking the inevitable any longer; she was about to meet his mother as his wife. She glanced back at her husband, but he was already out of the car and a second later had opened the car door for her.

'Welcome to Il Casa Maldini.' He gestured at the huge building with a wave of one hand, and, grasping her arm, helped her out of the low-slung sports car. 'A Ferrari was obviously not designed for a pregnant lady,' he said, grinning down at her as he swept an arm around her shoulders. 'From now on we will use the Mercedes.'

With some astonishment Kelly realised 'Il Casa Maldini' was actually engraved in the stone lintel above the great door. 'Some house,' she murmured. She tipped her head back and stared up at the building. Built in an open-ended rectangle, three storeys high, it was enormous. The ochre stuccoed walls gleamed golden in the pale winter sunshine.

'*Sì*, my family has owned the land around here for countless generations. Maldini is a very old and very much respected name,' he stated as he led her up the steps to the massive double doors, now magically opened by a small white-headed man.

In a flurry of introductions Kelly discovered the man's name was Aldo, his wife Maria was the cook; there were six more servants whose names she barely registered, and finally a young girl of about eighteen, Anna, who smiled shyly when Gianfranco introduced her to Kelly as her personal maid.

His mother appeared from a room at one side of the massive oak-panelled hall, and welcomed her son with a kiss on each cheek. Her greeting to Kelly was less demonstrative.

'I am sorry I missed the wedding, but it was so unexpected, so quick.' And her dark eyes, so uncannily like her son's, dropped down to Kelly's stomach and then quickly back to her face as she added, 'Welcome, Kelly; I know you *inglese* shake hands.' She held out a perfectly manicured hand.

'Thank you,' Kelly murmured. Hot colour scorching her cheeks, she took the hand offered her and hoped she had made the right noises, feeling intimidated by the woman, the line of servants and the overwhelming grandeur of the place.

Five minutes later, seated on a rather hard satin-backed sofa, Kelly looked around her in barely concealed awe. The furniture was all antique, and the magnificent marble fireplace was a masterpiece. But it was the ceiling that made her gasp, being exquisitely painted and depicting some kind of pastoral scene, with men and women lying around in various stages of undress, draped in vines and flowers.

'Kelly? What would you like?'

Kelly tore her gaze away from the stunning frescoes and glanced across at Gianfranco. He was standing by the fireplace, a thumb hooked in the hip-hugging band of his jeans, his other hand curved around a crystal glass half-full of what looked like whisky. Aldo the butler stood a few paces away from him.

'Alcohol is out for you, but coffee, or fresh juice? Aldo is waiting.'

'Oh, I'll have a cup of tea, please.' Kelly said the first thing that came into her head. She had not realised they were waiting for her.

'You are so English,' Gianfranco's mother said with a little laugh. 'I think you will find our ways quite strange.'

Aldo left after a quick command from Gianfranco, and then he turned to smile down at his mother. 'Rubbish, Mamma. Kelly will soon learn. With you to teach her, how could she not?' And the two of them shared a look of mutual understanding.

Watching, Kelly felt vaguely left out for a second, and not at all sure what it was she was supposed to learn from her very grand-looking, elegant mother-in-law.

Aldo returned and served the tea, while Gianfranco and his mother carried on a conversation in Italian, which effectively excluded Kelly. She knew some Italian, and had for the past few months been trying to learn more with the help of tapes, but they spoke too fast for Kelly to pick up more than a few words.

Suddenly dark eyes were turned on Kelly. 'Excuse us, Kelly, but my son and I have so much to catch up on, and I forget you do not speak our language.'

'That's perfectly all right,' Kelly said quietly, returning her teacup to the tray. 'I understand...' she hesitated '...Signora Maldini.' She had no idea how to address her new mother-in-law.

'Oh, please, as we are all going to live together, you must call me Carmela.'

Kelly smiled. 'Why, thank you, Carmela.'

'My pleasure, and now if you have finished your tea,

perhaps you would like Anna to show you the main part of the house, and then to your suite.' A bell was rung and in minutes Anna appeared at the door.

She was being sent to her room! Kelly almost laughed out loud. 'No, really—' she began to object, when Carmela cut in.

'In your delicate condition I am sure you will appreciate a rest in the afternoon. We dine at nine.'

Kelly glanced expectantly up at Gianfranco, sure he would object to what sounded to Kelly like a dismissal and offer to give her a guided tour himself. But instead he strolled across to where she sat and, reaching for her hand, urged her to her feet.

'Mamma is right. You go along with Anna. I have a few calls to make.' His lips brushed hers in a fleeting caress and, turning her towards the door, he patted her bottom. 'I'll see you soon.'

Hiding her disappointment, Kelly followed Anna as she dutifully pointed out the many reception rooms. Then she led Kelly up the grand staircase and along various corridors, pointing out Carmela's suite and Olivia's next to it. Kelly was slightly surprised at the mention of Olivia; she had not realised the woman lived here as well. The upper floor was the servants' quarters.

Gianfranco's suite was in the west wing of the house, and was more like an apartment, but without a kitchen. One huge bedroom and a large dressing room, two bathrooms, a comfortable sitting room and another slightly smaller bedroom. Standing in the middle of the sitting room, Kelly looked around, her mood lifting as she surveyed the fire burning brightly in the fireplace. It felt warm and welcoming. She sighed with relief and dismissed the maid.

One wall was lined with shelves and books. Old trophies were scattered around and, reading the inscriptions, Kelly realised they were for sailing. A large leather sofa and two armchairs were placed around the fireplace, and in one corner stood a writing table, in another a huge state-of-the-art television...

The main bedroom was equally inviting, with a large oak four-poster double bed, Kelly thought as she strolled into the dressing room on her way to the bathroom.

The dressing room was lined with cupboards on two sides, various chests of drawers and an ornate dressing table; all the furniture was large, but with the high ceilings everything was in proportion.

Kelly opened a wardrobe door and smiled. Anna had unpacked for her, and her clothes were lined alongside some of Gianfranco's. It was a comforting sight.

Two hours later, showered and changed into a soft blue wool skirt and matching blouse in blue and cream, Kelly curled up in a leather armchair and began to wonder where her husband had got to.

Getting up from the chair, she restlessly walked across to one of the elegant arched windows and looked out over the courtyard, the sweeping drive lined by Cypress trees, a beautifully tended Italian-style garden and, in the distance, the terracotta roofs of a village, all surrounded by mile upon mile of undulating cultivated land. She picked out row upon row of vines to one side, and vast olive groves.

A deep heartfelt sigh escaped her and she pressed her head against the cool glass of the window-pane. It was stupid, but true: she had not the nerve to go looking for her husband. The house was huge and her first impression on entering had been of gloom—the great hall, hung with ancient oil paintings of severe-looking men and women, a massive central staircase that ended with a galleried landing with numerous corridors off it.

Taking a deep breath, she straightened her shoulders.

Kelly, my girl, you are a married, pregnant adult woman, not a stupid adolescent, she lectured herself sternly. There was nothing stopping her going to look for her husband, and she turned on her heel. She was halfway across the room when the door opened and Gianfranco walked in.

'Sorry I was so long.' He slanted her a brief smile. 'But with everything that has happened I have neglected my work of late.'

'Sorry if I am an inconvenience,' nerves made her snap resentfully.

Collapsing on the sofa, Gianfranco held out a hand to her. 'Come here, my sensuous little wife,' he said softly, catching the flash of uncertainty she could not hide. 'No need to feel neglected, but I do have to work.'

Seated in the curve of his arm, Kelly listened as he explained.

'Apart from when I have to go to New York, I usually spend four days here over the weekend, when I attend to estate matters. The rest of the time I spend in my office in Rome. Obviously now I am a married man I will have to rethink my working practice, as I have no intention of leaving you alone more than I can help. I can easily work from here, and curtail my visits to Rome somewhat.'

'Why bother? I could stay in Rome with you.' She flashed him a brilliant smile; the thought of escaping his family for half of every week held great appeal.

'No, don't be ridiculous.' He clasped her shoulders and turned her around to face him. 'You need someone with you at all times in your condition.' His lips turned up in a self-satisfied smile. 'Me, and when I am not around Mamma and Olivia. The situation is ideal.'

Her mouth dropped open. He had to be kidding. But

before she could protest he had planted a swift kiss on her lips and got to his feet.

'I need a shower, *carissima*, and then...' his dark eyes gleamed wickedly '...we can both have a rest before dinner.'

CHAPTER SEVEN

IT WAS Saturday night and the guests were due to arrive in twenty minutes.

'What do you think, Anna?' she asked the young girl.

'*Bellissima.*' Anna grinned. 'Very elegant.'

'Thank you.' Kelly smiled back. The one good thing to come out of her first two weeks at the Casa Maldini was Anna. She was friendly, could speak a little English, and was eager to help. In fact, she had just spent half an hour doing Kelly's hair in an elaborate twist on the crown of her head with a few loose tendrils to frame her face. She watched the girl depart, then nervously she glanced once more at her reflection in the mirror. She so wanted to make a good impression on Gianfranco's friends.

The past two weeks had not been easy. She had expected some difficulty in adjusting to her husband's lifestyle, but she had never expected to feel so lonely. Aldo woke them in the morning at seven with coffee. Ten minutes later Gianfranco, washed and dressed, left her lying in bed while he started work, and if she was lucky she saw him at lunch. But most days it was eight in the evening before he reappeared.

Only once had he taken her out. With supreme efficiency he had whisked her into Verona and opened a bank account for her. Then he had registered her with his doctor and waited while she had a scan. On returning to the house he had dismissed her with a brief smile and told her he would see her later. By 'later' he meant over a very formal dinner with his mother and Olivia, or in bed.

Her lips quirked in the briefest of smiles; at least in bed she had his full attention, but it was the only place, she wryly conceded.

She had made a disturbing discovery about her husband. 'Count Gianfranco Maldini' the businessman was a totally different male animal from the Gianni she had fallen in love with. He was a workaholic, and he was spoilt rotten. His mother and Olivia waited on him hand and foot, as did all the staff, as if he was the Master of the Universe, and he took their adoration as his due. Their attitude to Kelly was not so friendly, though she had tried telling herself she must be mistaken when she thought she understood Olivia's sly comments in Italian. She had tried to convince herself she was being paranoid, but yesterday was a case in point.

Gianfranco had informed her in the morning that his mother and Olivia were going to take her shopping. When Kelly had asked him to go with her instead he had pleaded pressure of work, and then added, 'Mamma knows the right places to shop for a woman in your condition, whereas I haven't a clue.'

Sensitivity was obviously not his strong point. Kelly knew damn fine what he had meant. Probably the only clothes he had ever bought for women were of the designer variety from exclusive boutiques. Not maternity wear.

She'd been seething with resentment by the time she had returned from the shopping trip. Carmela and Olivia had overridden anything she had suggested with the comment that they knew best the acceptable way for pregnant women to dress in Italian society. Kelly had felt about two inches tall and shut up. Consequently she'd returned to the house with three of the most enormous dresses she'd ever clapped eyes on. However hard she tried, she could not convince herself Carmela and Olivia were looking after her best interests—in fact, quite the reverse.

She had said as much to Gianfranco, and he had gone all cold on her. He had told her she was jumping to ridiculous conclusions over a few misunderstood words, and then suggested it was her hormones playing up because of her pregnancy.

Walking out of the bedroom, Kelly knew she was pinning all her hopes on tonight; she wanted to fit in and make friends, but not at the loss of her pride and self-esteem. Which was why she was wearing the dress she had bought herself in England.

Taking a deep breath, she walked into the salon. Gianfranco had come down earlier. Olivia, looking stunning in a midnight-blue strapless and backless dress that clung to her every curve, was standing so close to him that they were almost touching.

Seeing her husband looking so incredibly handsome in a formal black dinner suit, smiling down at Olivia, gave Kelly a nasty jolt somewhere in the region of her heart. Straightening her shoulders, she walked into the middle of the room. 'Good evening.'

It was like watching a tableau unfold. Carmela was the first to notice Kelly, and when she did her perfectly plucked eyebrows rose in surprise.

Then Olivia laughed. 'Surely you're not wearing that?' she said, eyeing Kelly as if she had crawled out from under a rock.

Stiffening defensively, Kelly said, 'Yes, I am.' It was a perfectly plain silk-jersey black dress. Tiny diamanté straps supported a bodice that was cut in a straight line across her breasts. The material, cut on the bias, clung slightly from under her bust to just above her knees.

Kelly ignored the babble of Italian that ensued and glanced across at Gianfranco, waiting for him to smile to give her some support.

Gianfranco's dark eyes made a swift analytical survey of her stiffly held figure as he walked across to her. 'You look very nice, Kelly.' In fact, he thought she looked delectable, but he could see his mother's point of view.

'Damned with faint praise,' Kelly said drily as Gianfranco stopped and stared down at her from beneath hooded lids, his expression unreadable.

'No, really, you know you always look beautiful,' he said soothingly. 'But Mamma thought you would have worn one of the gowns she bought for you. She is of the opinion they are much more suitable for a wife during her confinement, and on matters of taste Mamma does know what is best. You would do well to take notice of her.'

Confinement! The old-fashioned term made Kelly bristle with indignation. Dear heaven, her arrogant husband and his sainted mother had got that right! she thought. She was beginning to feel more and more as if she was in jail. Well, to hell with the pair of them, tonight she was going to enjoy herself, if it was the last thing she did.

'I'll make your apologies, should it be necessary, while you change,' Gianfranco continued smoothly. 'But hurry.'

'No.'

One ebony brow arched. 'No! You refuse?'

She almost laughed, he looked so astounded. 'Got it in one.'

He caught her arm. 'Kelly, you're behaving foolishly. Now go upstairs and change,' he commanded, his dark eyes revealing his irritation.

Kelly glared up at him. 'I would look foolish if I wore any of the dresses I got yesterday. I'm five and a half months pregnant, not nine,' she snorted, nervous tension heightening her already rising temper. 'They make me look like an elephant. You should—you should see them.'

Gianfranco smiled when she began to splutter—a very

masculine grin. 'I see.' He let go of her arm. 'Female vanity I can understand,' he drawled mockingly.

She wanted to hit him; he was so damn condescending. But she never got the chance as Aldo announced the first guests had arrived. Carefully holding her temper under tight control, Kelly braced herself to meet a host of strangers.

It was nowhere near as bad as she had feared. Gianfranco's friends were not nearly as intimidating as his mother and sister-in-law, a mixture of local people and business acquaintances, and when Judy and Carlo Bertoni arrived Kelly could not hide her delight.

The buffet meal was exquisite, the conversation a mixture of English and Italian. Carmela sparkled and was the perfect hostess, and with Olivia quickly had a group of people hanging onto her every word.

Kelly, finding herself alone for a moment, began to relax. Gianfranco was at the other side of the room, deep in discussion with a group of men in what was obviously a male-only conversation.

Suddenly beside Kelly, Judy chuckled. 'Aren't you the dark horse?'

Kelly glanced at her and blushed.

Judy's eyes lit with amusement. 'Your local lad turned out to be Count Gianfranco Maldini—what a story! Come on, tell all. How did it happen?'

Kelly told her, ending with, 'In a way I have you to thank, because apparently when you told him at New Year that I was pregnant he came to look for me, and the rest, as they say, is history,' she quipped.

'That's great!' Judy asserted with a grin. 'But let me give you some advice; your Gianfranco has had plenty of women in his time, and he treated them all with a casualness you wouldn't believe. He is not the type for deep emotional commitment. But you're carrying his child, and

Italians love children, so make sure you make the most of it, and don't let him out of your sight.'

'Thanks, Judy.' Kelly forced a smile. She needed reminding of her husband's past women like a hole in the head, but that was Judy. 'But we are marr...' She never finished the sentence, as someone bumped into her and sent a shower of liquid down the front of her dress.

'Oh, I'm so sorry.' Olivia appeared in front of Kelly. 'I didn't see you there, and now your dress is ruined. How clumsy of me.' Kelly glanced up and the malevolence in the dark eyes that met hers froze her to the spot. 'Now you will *have* to change.'

Kelly couldn't believe the pettiness of it... But, overcome with embarrassment, as the dampness had made the fabric stick to her stomach, she did not want to make a scene. 'Yes,' she agreed.

With a hard glance at Olivia, Judy said, 'I'll come with you.'

Before they could move Gianfranco materialised at her side. His dark eyes swept down over her small body and the tell-tale damp patch over her stomach. 'What happened?' Everyone around them seemed to go silent.

'Nothing, really—an accident. Don't make a fuss.' She turned a deep, embarrassed shade of red.

Olivia laid a hand on his arm and he turned towards her as she said something in rapid Italian. The people around them laughed. Gianfranco grinned and, glancing back at Kelly, placed a hand in the small of her back. 'Hurry along, then.'

Kelly nodded without comprehending what had been said, and, with Judy at her side, exited the room.

'That bitch did that deliberately,' Judy remarked as they walked up the stairs. 'You're going to have to watch her.'

'No, really, it was an accident,' Kelly lied, not believing it for a second. 'These things happen.'

'That is not what she just told your husband,' Judy revealed bluntly. 'She joked it was the extra weight you were carrying—the Maldini heir—that made you stumble. Why do you think they all laughed?'

'No, I don't believe you,' Kelly said staunchly, defending Gianfranco and at the same time feeling incredibly hurt.

'Then I suggest you learn Italian—quick,' Judy declared drily.

Ignoring her, Kelly stripped off the dress, and after a brief visit to the bathroom to sponge down her stomach returned to the bedroom.

'Is this your bedroom?' Judy asked, glancing around and wandering into the sitting room, and finally the dressing room, where she flung open the wardrobe doors.

'Yes, of course.' Kelly followed her in and eyed her meagre supply of clothes with a jaundiced eye.

'You're in worse trouble than I thought,' Judy commented. 'This isn't the master suite of Casa Maldini. You do know that?' Judy lifted an enquiring eyebrow in Kelly's direction.

'No,' Kelly said with a dry smile. 'But I do know my own bedroom suite.'

'Maybe, but remember the magazine article I showed you, the luxurious master suite is in the other wing.'

'That's Olivia's,' Kelly muttered, pulling one of the new dresses from the wardrobe. The least offensive was a white muslin concoction sprigged with pink roses.

'Ah! So the black widow is firmly entrenched. I'm sorry to say this, Kelly, but you'd better get a grip. You are the top female in this house now, and it's time you started acting like it, or Olivia is going to walk all over you.'

'Really, Judy, you're being melodramatic.' She liked

Judy, but she knew her attitude towards men was manipulative; she only had to think of how she had used Kelly last summer to get her husband to agree to a full-time nanny.

Judy shook her head and sighed. 'Listen up, Kelly. There have been rumours about Olivia and Gianfranco for ages now, but it is also common knowledge Olivia can't have children. She was married for ten years to his brother and tried everything. If you are not very careful she will take over not just the master suite, but your husband and your child if you let her.'

'You have a vivid imagination,' Kelly muttered, lifting the dress prior to putting it over her head, but Judy's words had struck a chord.

'Oh, my God! You're never going to wear that!' Judy tore it from her hand. 'Where is your style, woman?'

Kelly sighed. 'Carmela and Olivia took me shopping and assured me this is what the best-dressed Italian mum-to-be wears.'

'Over my dead body,' Judy asserted and, rifling through the wardrobe, withdrew the winter-white cashmere dress that she'd worn for her wedding. 'Here, wear that—at least it has some style—and for heaven's sake think about what I have told you. You are far too trusting for your own good.'

The sound of music floated into the grand hall as the two girls made their way back downstairs. The dancing had started. Kelly glanced across the room just as Gianfranco took Olivia into his arms and started to dance.

Carlo Bertoni appeared and slid an arm around Judy. 'Where have you been? I missed you,' he declared, and as Kelly watched Judy smiled up into her husband's eyes.

'Helping the lady of the house change.'

'And very lovely you look.' Carlo smiled at Kelly. 'Gianfranco is a very lucky man.'

Kelly forced a smile. 'Thank you, Carlo.' But, watching Gianfranco dancing, with Olivia's arms now wrapped around his neck, she began to wonder how lucky she was herself. Somehow seeing the two so intimately together lent credence to Judy's outrageous suggestions. She felt sick to her stomach and was hit by a wave of such bitter jealousy she had to close her eyes for a moment.

Opening them again, she glanced around the room. It wasn't just Olivia who was ogling her husband, she noted. Gianfranco, with his great height and superbly muscled body, moved with a rhythm, a lithe, sexy elegance, which, combined with his dark good looks, attracted the appreciative eyes of almost every female present.

Gianfranco loved her, she told herself firmly. They were married, for heaven's sake. But a fluttering in her stomach reminded her she was pregnant and why he had married her. Then Gianfranco caught sight of her, his glorious eyes widening in delight, and she was reassured by the brilliant smile that he winged her way. She was worrying over nothing.

Kelly was wearing the dress she had married him in, and for a moment Gianfranco was stunned anew by how beautiful she looked. His wife, with her pale hair swept up on top of her head, her slender body ripening softly with his child. Yes, he had made the right decision marrying her, he congratulated himself, his chest swelling with pride. She was every inch a lady and, contrary to what he had been led to believe by married men of his acquaintance, marriage had made little difference to his life at all—except he had a warm and willing woman in his bed every night. Married life was good. His friends adored Kelly, the evening was a great success, and he wished the whole lot would leave so he could take her to bed.

The music stopped and he disengaged himself from his courtesy dance with his sister-in-law. He was stopped from claiming Kelly by Olivia's hand on his arm. He listened with barely concealed impatience to what she had to say, but when his mother joined in his attention was caught. Old loyalties vied with new, and slowly his dark brows drew together in a frown.

Kelly saw the frown, and she watched as he worked his way through the crowd towards her. Gianfranco reached for Kelly with a strong arm and pulled her to his side. 'I see you've changed,' he said, bending his dark head towards her, and under cover of apparently kissing her neck, said softly, 'Beautiful though you look, would it have been too much of a hardship to wear one of the gowns Mamma chose for you?'

'Yes,' she declared mutinously. She had already had this argument earlier, and she was not about to start trying to defend her choice again.

'Dance with me,' Gianfranco demanded. She stilled, and the large hand at her spine pulled her closer. 'Smile,' he suggested silkily, glittering dark eyes absorbing the defiance in her beautiful face. 'Or people might suspect that we are arguing.'

'Heaven forbid anyone would dare argue with you, Gianfranco,' she drawled sarcastically. And was punished by being kissed in a brief, hard kiss. Her nostrils flared on the disturbingly familiar scent of him, her body instantly melting in the circle of his arms. 'People are watching,' she said, her face flushing scarlet.

'So what? I am master in my own home,' he murmured against her ear as he guided her gently around the floor. 'You would do well to remember that. I am not used to the women in my life bending my ear about clothes,' he declared with all the aristocratic arrogance of his illustrious ancestors. 'It has got to stop—understand?'

Involuntarily Kelly flinched and missed a step, stung by the implied threat in his statement...

'Olivia was right, you are rather clumsy tonight,' he remarked.

Judy had not been lying! In that second Kelly wanted to thump him; her blue eyes flashed fire as they met his. 'And you are a blind chauvinist pig!' she whispered tightly.

Her sapphire eyes were magnificent when anger or passion aroused her, but he did not want to argue with her. 'Don't get upset, Kelly.' His gleaming dark eyes held hers. 'I will forgive you. It's probably your hormones playing up.'

Kelly pulled free just as the music stopped, but before she could speak Carmela tapped Gianfranco on the arm. 'The guests will soon be leaving.'

Half an hour later the last of the guests had left. Carmela declared the evening a great success and suggested they all have a nightcap. Kelly refused, said goodnight and made straight for the stairs.

Inside she was a seething mass of conflicting emotions. She loved Gianfranco, but he, by his own words, had admitted he had been laughing at her with Olivia. She couldn't believe he was so insensitive to her feelings. But then, she did not know him that well, as she was fast discovering.

Once in the bedroom, she quickly undressed, and in the bathroom she washed, then brushed out her hair, before slipping on a blue satin nightgown. She grimaced slightly—it was getting a little snug—and walked back into the bedroom.

After an instant's hesitation at seeing Gianfranco, she continued towards the bed.

'Rather a hasty exit, Kelly,' he opined hardly. 'It wouldn't have hurt you to share a nightcap with Mamma.'

'I thought I'd leave you to it, then you could all have a good laugh at me,' she snapped.

In the process of divesting himself of his clothes he stopped and faced her, his dinner suit discarded and his fingers lingering on the last button of his shirt.

'What exactly do you mean by that?' He shrugged off his shirt and stood before her in just black silk boxers. His dark eyes narrowed intently on her pale face. 'You have been in a strange mood for the past hour.'

'Maybe because I don't like being told what to wear, or being ordered to change.'

Gianfranco stilled, his broad shoulders tensing. 'Maybe you should learn some courtesy to my mother, when she has very generously tried to help you,' he opined bluntly.

'Maybe you should learn some courtesy to me, your *wife*,' she snarled, the events of the evening finally getting on top of her. 'Like when your sister-in-law tipped her drink all over me and apologised. Yet, according to Judy, when you appeared she told you it was my clumsiness and you all had a jolly good laugh.'

A dark stain of red ran along his high cheekbones. At least he had the grace to blush, which was something, Kelly thought bitterly. Thoroughly fed-up, she did not want to argue with him, she wanted him to hold her in his arms and reassure her of his love, and instead he was staring at her with eyes as cold as ice.

'Everyone laughed; as the host, I smiled in agreement with my guests, the correct thing to do,' he said with chilling politeness. 'But you are being ridiculous, Kelly. I have known Olivia a lot longer than you and she would not lie.'

'No? You're inferring that I would?' Kelly shot back at him in outrage.

'Yes—no.' For once her indomitable husband had to struggle for words. 'You were probably mistaken, a woman in your condition.'

'If you mention my condition once more, so help me I will flatten you,' she screeched tempestuously.

His jaw clenched. 'Contain yourself, Kelly, such temper cannot be good for you or the baby.'

Too angry to bother guarding her tongue, Kelly flared, 'And you supporting Olivia over your wife is? The woman sleeps in the master suite and her husband has been dead over three years. But then maybe she is waiting for the new master to take his place, or perhaps you already have,' she snarled, shaking with anger.

Gianfranco went rigid, tension emanating from him in waves. Hooded black eyes surveyed her with a look of such simmering rage that she involuntarily stepped back, afraid of a physical attack. Her anger vanished. She knew she had gone too far. What on earth had possessed her to throw Judy's coarse rumours in his face?

'You do well to retreat, Kelly. If you were not carrying my child I would make you pay for such a slanderous slur on your husband and a woman who has done you no harm but welcomed you into the family home.'

Kelly had never seen Gianfranco so angry; his eyes were flat and cold, and somehow that frightened her. He caught her shoulders and she trembled. His tanned near-naked body had the familiar devastating effect on Kelly. He was so close she had trouble breathing. 'Sorry,' she murmured, completely subjugated by his towering presence.

Gianfranco saw the fear in her deep blue eyes and checked himself. She in turn infuriated and enchanted him, and if he could get his hands on whoever it was putting such stupid ideas in her head he would strangle them. 'Tell me, who has been filling your head with such rubbish?' he demanded, staring down at her, noting the panicked bounding of her heart and the rise and fall of her breasts against the soft satin covering them.

'No one.' Kelly lowered her eyes and stared at his broad chest. 'It probably is just my hormones playing up,' she offered as an excuse, and perhaps it was, she told herself, filled with shame at what she had implied. She had sounded like the worst kind of jealous wife. But she was not going to betray Judy. 'When Anna showed me around I knew Olivia…' She trailed off.

Gianfranco breathed a sigh of relief and pulled her into his arms. Hormones he could understand. He brushed his lips across her smooth brow in a tender gesture. 'Perhaps I should have explained earlier, but you have to understand Olivia was devastated by the death of her husband Alfredo—my brother. We all were. But Olivia had a nervous breakdown and was ill for over a year, and, although she appears very confident and in control, she is still very fragile. She is family, so naturally Mamma and I look after her.'

Kelly was feeling worse by the minute. 'Oh, how terrible for her.' Her soft heart was touched.

'Yes, *cara*,' he murmured softly. 'In a way you have everything that was once hers.'

Her body was shivering in the protective circle of his strong arms, but not with cold. She loved him; she would do anything for him. She could not bear him to be angry with her, and yet she couldn't help it. 'But not you.' The words just popped out.

He chuckled, a deep, husky sound, and moulded her against him. 'No, never me, but I'm flattered you're jealous, *cara*.' One lean, strong hand cupped her chin, his dark eyes intent on her lovely face. 'But you are now married to the present count, and not only that, you are pregnant with probably the next one. Something that Olivia would have killed for when Alfredo was alive but it was not to be. So try to make allowances for her, hmm?'

She nodded her head, and his mouth, hot and urgent, covered her own as he kissed her with a long, lingering sexuality.

Kelly tried to make allowances, she really did… But it wasn't easy.

Olivia's hurtful comments whenever Gianfranco was not around, her hints that they had been lovers, were like water torture, slowly draining all Kelly's confidence and self-esteem. She tried to talk to Gianfranco but he dismissed her fears, sometimes with a laugh, occasionally with cold disdain, which hurt her even more, but usually with a kiss. But sex was no longer enough for Kelly. She needed more, she needed her husband's support, and when it was not forthcoming she grew more miserable and withdrawn by the day.

Kelly gave up mentioning Olivia to her husband, and with no one to turn to she struggled vainly against her doubts and fear. Gianfranco told her he adored her, made love to her, but he never made any attempt to find out how her mind worked. He treated her like a treasured pet. Sometimes when a sense of hopelessness overwhelmed her she wandered into the little-used rooms of the great house and gave in to her growing sense of isolation and misery, crying herself sick. It said it all that nobody even missed her…

When Gianfranco mentioned two weeks later that he was leaving for America the next day, Kelly wanted to object. She looked at him across the width of their private sitting room. He was handsome, powerful, autocratic, but she realised bitterly, there was no point. He did what he wanted when he wanted; he was not asking her approval, simply telling her, and she simply agreed. In a brief moment of clarity her melancholy lifted enough for her to wonder where the cartwheeling, kick-boxing, bright young career-minded woman of last summer had gone. But Gianfranco's smile as he took her in his arms and kissed her made the image fade.

Within hours of Gianfranco departing, Carmela was called away to stay with a sick friend in Verona, and Kelly was left with only Olivia for company.

At dinner that night Olivia showed her true colours. She lashed into Kelly, telling her that she was gold-digging little slut and Gianfranco cared nothing for her, only the child. When Kelly tried to respond Olivia actually threw a glass of wine over her.

Running from the room, Kelly seriously wondered if the woman was mentally stable at all. She had seen madness in her eyes. Perhaps all her hateful comments and innuendoes were the work of a twisted mind. Paradoxically it made Kelly feel much better. Gianfranco was her husband, and Olivia could not hurt Kelly unless she let her. The easiest way was to avoid Olivia altogether. With that thought in mind, Kelly informed Aldo she would be eating in her suite until the master returned.

Gianfranco phoned the next morning, and after assuring himself Kelly was fine he asked to speak to his mother. Kelly told him she had gone to visit a sick friend. She knew he assumed she meant for a few hours, but didn't elaborate. She was so pleased to hear the sound of his voice she wanted nothing to spoil their rapport.

Kelly heaved a sigh of relief as she watched Olivia drive away the next afternoon to visit Rome. Alone in the house, without Olivia's hateful presence, Kelly thought she might get to like it, but, as a woman who had always been active, she found being waited on hand and foot slightly irksome.

Making a determined effort to get over the misery that was blighting her pregnancy and could not be good for the baby, Kelly took to going for long walks exploring the surrounding countryside. One day she stopped off at the local bar in the nearest village for a refreshing glass of lemonade before returning to the Casa Maldini. Gradually her confidence returned. She even found the nerve to drive the Mercedes that Gianfranco had put at her disposal, and travelled further afield to go shopping. Usually Anna accompanied her.

Ten days later her mother-in-law returned, full of apologies for her absence, and Olivia turned up a couple of hours later.

The next day Gianfranco arrived. Kelly watched him slide out from behind the wheel of his sports car. He was dressed casually in a black leather jacket, black roll-neck sweater, and wickedly skin-tight jeans. With his hair falling over his brow she was vividly reminded of Gianni and the fun they had had with the motorbike, and her heart turned over with love. She looked down at herself, and a regretful sigh escaped her; nothing could hide the fact she was over six months pregnant. But she had dressed with care in black trousers and a bright red and black tunic, and she knew she looked good.

Kelly glanced up and Gianfranco's dark eyes met hers, and in unison they smiled. He stepped forward and crushed her in his arms, kissing her with a hungry passion that wiped all the doubt and fear from her mind.

Over the next two days they made love often. For Kelly a kind of radiant hope began to break through the suspicion and misery of the last few weeks. Gianfranco spent most of the day closeted in his study, but his nights were all hers.

The third night, Kelly dressed in black jersey silk harem pants, with a matching top lavishly covered in multicoloured embroidery. She looked great and felt even better. Full of confidence, she hummed a tune as she descended the stairs into the hall.

Gianfranco always dressed first, and then went downstairs for his usual whisky and soda before dinner, but tonight he had delayed long enough to make love to her in the shower, which was the reason for her good humour.

Olivia was standing in the hall looking her usual immaculate self in a black dress.

'Hi, Olivia,' Kelly said with a polite smile.

'Smile while you have the chance—you won't for much longer,' Olivia sneered, and swept into the dining room in front of Kelly.

A bit of Kelly's renewed confidence slipped as she walked into the room.

It slipped a lot further over dinner. The conversation was stilted, and Gianfranco sat for the most part in a brooding silence. When Kelly said anything he replied in monosyllables, and she was heartily glad when the meal was over. She made her excuses and was the first to leave the table. There was something about this house, she thought fancifully as she walked out into the gloomy hall, that reeked of dark deeds and hidden passions.

'Wait, Kelly.' Gianfranco grasped her arm. 'Come into the study a minute; we need to talk.'

'You've got that right,' she said with feeling. 'What the hell was all that about?' she demanded, following him into the study.

Gianfranco stopped by the desk and swung around to face her. He looked at Kelly, with her blonde hair falling smooth as silk to her shoulders and her blue eyes fixed on him, looking as innocent as sin! He wanted her as he had never wanted any other woman, but she had to realise as his wife she had certain standards to maintain. He was a very busy man, with an estate and a financial empire to run. He expected his home life to proceed like clockwork, and he didn't have time to oversee it himself. He should have had this conversation with Kelly weeks ago, but in the time they spent together she knocked every sensible thought out of his head and all he could think of was making love to her. She drove him crazy, probably always would, but it was time he laid down some ground rules.

'So talk,' Kelly said, glancing across at her husband, looking magnificently male and moody. 'I don't know why you're being so brooding.' She gave a little laugh.

His eyes narrowed, not a glimmer of a smile softening his saturnine features. 'Kelly, as my wife you have a certain position to uphold in the community, and there are certain things that are not acceptable.'

Her smooth brow pleated in a frown; he had to be joking. 'Like picking my nose?' she joked, hoping to lighten the atmosphere. But she failed...

CHAPTER EIGHT

IGNORING her attempt at humour, Gianfranco said, 'It has been brought to my attention that in my absence you were seen in the village on your own in the local bar.'

'So? I was tired and I stopped for a glass of lemonade.' She didn't see his point.

'Kelly, that is not suitable behaviour for my wife, nor is speeding around the countryside in a car with one of the servants. Could you imagine my mother or Olivia ever doing such a thing? They were horrified when they found out,' he told her, a grim smile parting his firm lips. 'I can't be here all the time, and when I am away I would be obliged if you would try and listen to their advice. Olivia assures me she did try to tell you what was expected of the lady of the house, and warned you more than once about your behaviour. You ignored her.'

His comment was like a red rag to a bull. Now she knew what Olivia had meant earlier about wiping the smile off her face. 'That is amazing, considering your mother wasn't here almost the whole time you were away. As for Olivia, apart from calling me a tramp the first night you left, she shot off to Rome the next day. In fact, if it hadn't been for Anna I wouldn't have spoken to a soul until your mother came back the day before you.'

He folded his arms across his broad chest. 'Rubbish.' His disdainful smile had been replaced by a stern, fixed stare. 'I told them to look after you.'

Kelly stared at him. 'You arrogant, conceited, pompous oaf!' she said, her hands on her hips. 'If you could hear yourself.' She shook her head, her blonde hair flying around her face. 'You sound like you're lecturing a child.'

'Not a child, Kelly, but you.' He gave her a cold smile. 'And you do have a tendency to act as a child.'

'Sorry,' she shot back sarcastically, 'but you have the tendency to act like God.'

His hands fell to his sides and he leant back against the desk and stuffed them in his pockets. 'And you have a tendency to, I wouldn't say lie, exactly, but exaggerate,' he drawled cynically. 'I called you every day and you never once mentioned you were alone. Odd, wouldn't you say?' One dark brow arched sardonically.

She looked at him; he was standing with his hands in his pockets, tightening the fine wool of his trousers across his thighs. He was a virile, sexy man and she loved him, but she did not have to listen to this.

'Nowhere near as odd as having a husband who does not believe a word I say,' she opined bitterly, and, spinning on her heel, she left, with tears blinding her eyes. She'd had such hopes for their reunion, but nothing had changed.

Midnight and Kelly was lying wide-awake in bed, tensely waiting for Gianfranco. She heard the sound of the shower running, then silence. The bedroom door opened and closed. Dry mouthed, her stomach swirling with a mixture of desire and dismay, Kelly watched him through the thick screen of her lashes as he walked towards the bed. He was so splendidly male; his naked olive-skinned body gleamed in the rays of moonlight shining through the window. He was a wonderful lover, but however much she tried to ignore the fact she knew in her heart it was no longer enough. A marriage needed more than sex—like sharing each other's hopes, and fears, trust. She opened her mouth to say as much when he slipped into bed beside her, only to have it covered with a tender kiss.

'Sorry, Kelly.' He gathered her in his arms. 'Mamma told me you were right; forgive me.' Quickly divesting her of her nightgown, he gathered her gently in his arms.

Held close against his naked length, she sighed and forgave him. He made love to her with an aching tenderness that brought tears to her eyes. It was only afterwards that doubt reared its ugly head again. Gianfranco believed his mother, believed Olivia, but his wife was another matter entirely. And the thought hurt so much that sleep was a long time coming.

'*Buon giorno, cara.*'

Kelly's eyes fluttered open. Gianfranco was standing by the bed, wearing a grey three-piece suit. He looked exactly what he was, an incredibly handsome, dynamic businessman, but more importantly her husband, and she stretched and smiled up at him.

'Sorry to wake you, sweetheart, but I am leaving shortly for Rome. It looks as if I will probably have to stay a night or two, and I couldn't leave without kissing my wife goodbye.' He sent her a slow, teasing smile that made her heart beat faster in her chest. 'Miss me and be good. I'll call tonight.' Swooping down, he pressed a long, hard kiss on her softly parted lips.

Dazed by his kiss, she didn't get the chance to object before he had left.

Nothing had really changed, she thought sadly as she wandered aimlessly through the great hall the next morning.

Aldo called her to the telephone. It was Judy Bertoni. Glad to hear a familiar voice, Kelly jumped at the chance when Judy suggested she drive over to Desenzano for lunch and a bit of shopping. Apparently she had opened the house by the lake early, as her father-in-law was ill and the family were staying in Italy to be near him.

Kelly told Carmela where she was going, and, by the time she arrived in Desenzano two hours later, her melancholy mood had lifted a little. Judy greeted her, and seeing the garden where she'd first met Gianfranco, when she'd thought he was a thief, brought a smile to her face.

Driving back towards the Casa Maldini at seven o'clock that night, Kelly was in a much better frame of mind. The trunk of the Mercedes was stuffed full of things for the baby, and a few for herself. She had hardly used the allowance Gianfranco had given her. She only hoped he wasn't mad at how much she had spent today, with Judy's encouragement.

The next thing she saw was the headlights of a car coming straight for her. She swerved violently, and stopped. The seatbelt cut into her stomach like a knife, but prevented her from knocking herself out against the windscreen. With her heart pounding she looked around—the other car had gone. Shaking with shock, she felt her brow. Not much of a bump, she consoled herself, but it was some minutes before she stopped trembling enough to drive on.

By the time she reached the Casa Maldini, she felt ill. Getting out of the car, she instructed Aldo to bring in her purchases and went straight upstairs. A visit to the bathroom confirmed her worst fear: she was bleeding.

Carefully she walked back into the bedroom, and Anna was just entering with some packages. Kelly managed to tell her she needed the doctor, and in seconds Carmela was there and helping her undress and get into bed.

The next few hours were a nightmare. Dr Credo arrived, and after a thorough investigation decided Kelly should stay where she was. The baby appeared to be safe, but he was not taking any chances. Bedrest for at least the next week, and he would check every morning.

* * *

'*Idiota,* must you always be such an impulsive fool?' Gianfranco's voice woke her from a shallow sleep.

She opened her eyes and looked up to see him standing by the bed. He was wearing a dark suit, a white silk shirt open at the throat, a tie hanging loose around his neck. His black hair was rumpled, and his dark eyes were shooting sparks.

'You're back,' she said inanely.

'Back? Of course I'm back. I left a room full of people in the middle of some crucial negotiations and hired a helicopter. What do you expect when I am told you drive the car almost in a ditch and nearly kill yourself and the baby? Are you mad or just plain stupid? What on earth possessed you to drive to Desenzano after Olivia told you not to? Do you have a death wish or something?' Staccato-voiced, like a machine-gun firing, he let rip with the questions.

'And hello to you, too,' Kelly murmured, closing her eyes against the tears that threatened to fall. Olivia again! Why wasn't she surprised? But this time she was not about to argue; she needed all her strength for her baby. She was finally accepting that Gianfranco had about as much sensitivity as a rhinoceros—he was raving at her like a lunatic when she could have done with some tender loving care.

'Damn it, look at me when I am talking to you.'

Kelly, clutching the coverlet with two hands over her chest, opened eyes awash with tears and looked up.

Gianfranco stilled, his face turning grey beneath the tan. What in God's name was he doing yelling at her? She looked shocked and she was crying. He had never seen Kelly cry and it broke his heart. 'Kelly,' he began in a voice that shook.

'What on earth is going on in here?' Carmela walked into the bedroom. 'Really, Gianfranco, you're shouting so loud the servants can hear you.' With a furious glance at

her son she sat down on the side of the bed and, brushing
Kelly's hair from her brow with an elegant beringed hand,
added, 'Take no notice of him, child, he doesn't know what
he is saying.'

Kelly was so stunned by her mother-in-law's intervention
that she couldn't say a word.

'You go to sleep, as the doctor ordered, and don't
worry—you and the baby are going to be fine.' Then, turning blistering eyes back to her son, she got to her feet and
pushed his arm. 'As for you, go and get a drink and calm
down.'

Gianfranco hesitated for a second, his night-black eyes
seeking Kelly's, but she avoided his gaze, and, spinning on
his heel, he left the room.

Kelly's whole attitude changed overnight. The shock of
the accident and the realisation that, but for the grace of
God, it could have been much worse and she might have
lost the baby filled her mind to the exclusion of everything
else. When Gianfranco walked in the next morning she listened to his apology for yelling; she even half-believed him
when he said it had been because he was so terrified of
losing her it had made him angry. But she refused to get
excited. The doctor had said no excitement, no stress, and
plenty of bedrest.

When he took her in his arms and kissed her she responded as usual, but with a slight indefinable restraint.
When he told her the doctor had said no sex until after the
baby was born she accepted it, and when he suggested he
sleep in the other bedroom, so as not to disturb her, she
accepted that as well.

A kind of lethargy enfolded her, all she wanted to do
was rest and take care of her child. Gianfranco was kind-
ness itself. He took her out to dinner with friends, and he
was solicitous of her welfare. That was when she saw him.

His business kept him in Rome, and a trip to Australia to check out a vineyard there took up most of his time. Olivia's sly comments no longer bothered her—her baby was more important than the petty jealousies of a widowed sister-in-law, Kelly told herself.

When she called Gianfranco in Rome one night, and Olivia answered the telephone, Kelly listened as Gianfranco explained without being asked that Olivia was there to shop, so naturally she was staying in the family apartment. Kelly responded with, 'Yes, of course.' Her only interest was her baby.

It was Easter weekend that finally broke her out of her lethargy. The sun was shining, spring had arrived and, eight months pregnant, Kelly finally slipped on the white and rose muslin dress Carmela had bought her. A wry smile curved her lips when she caught sight of her reflection in the mirror. It seemed an age ago when she had complained about it, but now it actually looked quite good, because she filled it.

'*Cara*. Are you ready?' Gianfranco walked into the bedroom, and stopped.

Kelly was standing by the mirror, smiling, and he didn't think he had ever seen her looking more beautiful. She was wearing a white and pink loose-fitting dress with a wide floppy collar, with her long silver-gilt hair falling way past her shoulders. She reminded him of a Gainsborough painting, and he had to stuff his hand in his pocket to control the instant tightening in his groin. He hadn't dared sleep with her because he did not trust himself not to make love to her. Instead he was working like the devil, so when the time came he would be able to take a long break with his wife and child. Only one more month, and then another few weeks and she would be his again.

Telling himself to get his mind above his waist, he

walked across and took her arm. Kelly smiled up at him, and he dropped a brief kiss on her lips—the most he dared to allow himself. 'Come on, I'll take you down to dinner.'

With Gianfranco's arm around her Kelly relaxed into the hard warmth of his body, feeling once more the familiar rush of happiness his touch evoked.

When he stroked her stomach with his free hand, and bent his dark head towards her and said huskily, 'Not long now; I can hardly wait,' she actually trembled slightly, and felt loved.

Dinner was pleasant. Carmela even complimented Kelly on her appearance. Given that she had chosen the dress, it was a bit of a back-handed compliment, but it raised Kelly's spirits anyway. It was over coffee the bomb dropped...

Carmela started it. 'All of Rome society attends. We always go as a family, and stay the night. It is the biggest charity gala of the year. Probably because after the restrictions of Lent are over everyone wants to celebrate.'

'Sounds good.' Kelly grinned; she felt better than she had in months. 'I can't wait.'

She listened as Gianfranco explained he had to attend it, as it was expected of him, and all the reasons why Kelly could not. It was too far to travel in her condition—they couldn't take any chances with the baby. They would only be gone the one night, and Anna and all the staff had strict instructions to look after her.

He had to be joking! Kelly thought. Next weekend, of all weekends! It was her birthday on the Saturday!

Olivia smiled at Gianfranco. 'If Kelly is worried about being on her own, I don't mind missing the gala and staying with her.'

'That's very generous of you,' Gianfranco said with a

beaming smile for Olivia. 'But not necessary—is it, Kelly?' he asked, his dark eyes capturing Kelly's.

'No. I'll be perfectly all right with Anna.' At least Anna genuinely seemed to like her. She was no longer sure of *any* of her dinner companions...

It suddenly hit her that for the past few months she had been married to Gianfranco her lifestyle had changed dramatically; with a few exceptions she had agreed to everything he wanted, so unsure was she of her position as his wife. He, on the other hand, had made no compromise whatsoever in his lifestyle. His trips abroad, his frequent stays in Rome... In a flash of blinding clarity she saw it all, and did not like what she had become. Bit by bit, her confidence in herself as a woman had been chipped away. Without a murmur she'd accepted separate bedrooms, because he said it would be better for her. How often in the night had she awakened, alone in the huge bed, full of fear at the enormity of giving birth? She would have liked the comfort and protection of Gianfranco's arms around her. It didn't have to be sex...

She recalled how insatiable he had been when they were first married. He was a very virile man with a great sex drive. What had Judy said? *'He is not the type for deep emotional commitment...don't let him out of your sight.'* Perhaps she should have listened...

Kelly sat up straighter in the hard-backed dining chair; seated at Gianfranco's right, she flicked a look at his chiselled profile—darkly masculine and supremely confident. He also looked tired. Perhaps he had been unfaithful. How would she know, stuck in the country? All her doubts suddenly resurfaced in her head.

'You're sure?' Gianfranco said quickly, his black eyes narrowing on her pale face with an intensity that seemed to want to read her mind.

Kelly forced a smile to her stiff lips. 'Positive.' She placed her hand over his on the table. 'Now, if you will excuse me.' She squeezed his hand before letting go. 'I'm rather tired.' Pushing back her chair, she flinched as Gianfranco leapt immediately to his feet and took her arm, helping her up.

She needed breathing space, time to marshal her thoughts, but Gianfranco insisted on taking her to her room and helping her undress. She saw the desire flare in his dark eyes as he lifted her nightgown over her head and smoothed it down over her shoulders, his large hand lingering tenderly on her stomach.

Over the past few weeks she had deliberately suppressed the memories of what it felt like to be in his arms, wild with passion, her whole being centred on him, drowning in desire. Now, at the worst possible moment, heat flooded through her, and she trembled. She wanted to be angry with him, but she couldn't. He would remember her birthday, Kelly told herself; even he could not be that insensitive. She was worrying over nothing.

'I know, I know, Kelly,' Gianfranco murmured, and took her in his arms and kissed her long and gently, his dark eyes narrowed intently on her face. 'But it won't be for much longer.' A rueful smile twisted his firm lips, and, taking her hand, he pressed it hard against his aroused flesh. 'It is a lot worse for me, I can assure you.' He groaned. 'But as soon as we can I am going to take you away for a long holiday.'

He wanted her and he loved her—he must do, because she couldn't bear it if he didn't. 'There is no need for us both to suffer,' she whispered, her slender fingers deftly unfastening his trousers.

'No. No. It's not fair. I can do nothing for you; the doctor was quite explicit.'

Kelly simply smiled, her heart racing, and very soon Gianfranco was saying, 'Yes. Yes.'

Kelly slept soundly that night, totally reassured Gianfranco did love her, and she went on thinking it until she watched the Mercedes vanish out of sight early the next Saturday morning.

Tears filled her eyes as she made her way back upstairs to her bedroom and, curling up in a ball on the bed, she let them fall. Today was her birthday, and she had been so sure Gianfranco would remember, stay with her. In her mind it had become a crucial test of his commitment. She had been wrong...

The house was full of servants and yet she had never felt so totally and utterly alone in her whole life. She cried, great racking sobs that shook her whole body; she wept until she had no tears left. It was a nagging pain in her lower back some time later that finally forced her to sit up on the bed. Kelly rubbed her tear-swollen eyes; wallowing in self-pity was no good, for her or the baby.

At ten o'clock the same night Kelly could delay no longer. The pains had started mid-afternoon but she had rested and eaten dinner and tried to pretend it wasn't happening. It was too soon...

Aldo drove her to the hospital in Verona, and Anna accompanied her. Kelly was grateful for her help. Anna held her hand and reassured her when the pain was almost unbearable, and at five to one in the morning Kelly gave birth to a healthy baby girl with a striking mop of ginger hair. In the euphoria of holding her baby in her arms, she could forgive for a moment the fact Gianfranco had not been with her when she needed him. And in the next hour she forgot about everything as the doctor and nurse fussed over her.

The sound of hushed voices wakened Kelly, and her eyes fluttered open. Groggily she glanced around. She was in a private room, and then immediately she remembered, her gaze flying to the side of the bed and the crib.

Gianfranco, tall, dark and incredibly handsome, was at the foot of the crib, still dressed in the formal dinner suit he had obviously worn for the charity gala. His chiselled features looked oddly severe. His mother was standing beside him, but his whole concentration was fixed on the baby.

He was here at last, Kelly thought, her heart swelling with love and pride, and was about to speak to let him know she was awake.

'It's ginger.' He glanced at his mother, an expression of complete amazement on his handsome face, and then back to the baby.

Kelly heard him, and something in her rebelled. 'She is a girl, not an it,' she murmured, hauling herself up into a sitting position.

'Kelly, Kelly, *mia cara*.' Gianfranco dashed to her side, and his dark eyes, blazing with emotion, caught and held hers.

'Kelly, she is beautiful; a perfect little girl. Thank you, thank you. I can't begin to tell you how sorry I am I wasn't here.' Sitting down on the side of the bed, he cupped her face in his strong hands and scattered dozens of frantic kisses on her eyes, her brow, her nose, and finally he covered her mouth.

A slight cough broke them apart. Carmela said, 'Congratulations, Kelly! She is perfect, and now I think I should leave you three alone to get used to being a family.' And to Kelly's surprise she actually bent down and kissed her cheek before departing.

'You don't mind she is not a boy?' Kelly asked Gianfranco as he got up and went back to the crib, staring at his child as if he had never seen a baby before.

He turned his dark eyes gleaming with pride. 'Of course not, *cara*.' His firm lips turned back against brilliant white teeth in the most magnificent smile Kelly had ever seen. 'The next one will probably be a boy.' His comment gave Kelly pause for thought, but then the doctor arrived.

'So how is the new mother now?' Dr Credo asked jovially, standing by the bed. Taking Kelly's wrist in his hand, he took her pulse.

'Fine.' She smiled up at him while the nurse deftly slipped another pillow behind her back.

'Good. You gave us a bit of a scare earlier. Three weeks early—well, one week early really, as two weeks either side of the given date is acceptable. But I am happy to say the baby is perfect. You, on the other hand, are going to have to take care. You haemorrhaged a little after the birth, so we are going to keep you here for a week.' Letting go of her wrist, he turned and took Gianfranco's arm and led him to the far side of the room, talking softly.

Kelly heard the raised voice of her husband and glanced across at him. He was standing, broad shoulders taut, his hands curled into fists at his sides, his face grey beneath the tan, the strong features rigid with some intolerable emotion. His dark gaze moved back to her face, his eyes widening as though he had suddenly realised some great truth. He was a father, and the thought crossed her mind that he did not look particularly ecstatic, more shell-shocked, but she didn't care, as the nurse handed her her baby.

She gazed down in awe at the beautiful, tiny face, the shock of bright red hair, and she was filled with an overwhelming love. She hugged the child to her breast, and pressed the lightest of kisses to the baby's cheek. 'Anna,' she whispered. Then, with the assistance of the nurse, the baby was suckling at her breast.

When the doctor and nurse left, Gianfranco slowly returned to the bedside, his dark eyes narrowing intently. A lump rose in his throat; his lids came down over tear-filled dark eyes, hiding his thoughts.

'Look, Gianfranco, she's feeding,' Kelly murmured, wanting to share the magic moment. 'Isn't she gorgeous?'

He lifted his lashes, making no attempt to hide the moisture in his eyes. 'Yes, you both are,' he said huskily, and, sinking down on the bed beside Kelly, he reached out a finger and gently traced the curve of the baby's cheek, the curve of Kelly's breast.

He watched mother and child, and silently thanked God for their safety. No thanks to him, he thought, for once in his life completely humbled. The information Dr Credo had revealed to him had shocked him to his soul. He had never known Kelly's mother had died in childbirth, but then he had never asked, he castigated himself. Dr Credo had said she did not like talking about it. Apparently he had contacted her own doctor in England for her notes, and that was how he knew. He had assured Gianfranco it was not genetic. But it didn't make Gianfranco feel any better.

'Do you want to hold her?' Kelly asked, pulling the soft cotton of her gown back over her luscious breast. She lifted her head, her eyes, glowing like sapphires, brimming with happiness, seeking his. She chuckled at the flicker of fear she saw in the dark depths that met hers.

'Come on, she won't bite,' she said simply. Nothing could spoil her delight in her child, and she watched as Gianfranco very carefully took the child from her arms.

They looked good together: the broad-shouldered dark-haired father cuddling the infant in his strong arms, a totally besotted look on his handsome face as he stared down at the baby.

'She has my father's hair, but she definitely has your eyes,' Kelly bubbled on. 'I thought we might call her Anna

Louise. You picked Alfredo for a boy and said I could choose if it was a girl. So what do you think? Anna after Anna, who has been a good friend to me, and was such a help last night, and Louise after my mother.'

'Anna Louise is perfect,' Gianfranco said quietly. He could hardly object to his child being named after a servant when the said servant was the only friend Kelly had made in their brief marriage. He had been partying the night away when Kelly had needed him. In all his thirty-one years he had never felt so inadequate—a new experience for him. But he made a silent vow that from now on his first priority was his wife and child.

The nurse entered and took the infant from Gianfranco and placed her in the crib.

'Rest, Signora Maldini,' she said, and, turning back to Kelly, gently eased out a pillow to allow Kelly to lie back down in the bed.

'Yes,' Kelly sighed. 'I am rather tired.' Her long lashes fluttered down. She smiled as she felt the soft brush of Gianfranco's mouth against her own. 'Nice,' she murmured, and slept.

When Kelly awoke three hours later the first of the flowers were delivered, and by evening the nurse complained they were running out of vases. From Gianfranco came dozens of red roses; the card read simply *'Thank you, my love'* and his name. From the staff, from friends…half from people Kelly didn't know. But the headily scented blooms that filled the air completely eclipsed the faint hospital smell.

It was the best week of her life. Gianfranco visited morning and night, and he presented her with an exquisite diamond bracelet. For our daughter, he had said, and kissed her. He brought Anna with him one morning, which delighted Kelly, and on another Olivia, which did not. When

Gianfranco was talking to the nurse Olivia got her dig in. 'You couldn't even do this right—we wanted a boy.'

Kelly ignored her; she was so happy. Judy Bertoni arrived, and let drop she was pregnant again, and the two girls arranged, with Gianfranco's tacit agreement, to spend a few days' shopping when the baby was a bit older.

Apart from the doctor, all the staff spoke only Italian, and much to Kelly's satisfaction her own Italian had improved dramatically, thanks to her tapes.

The following Saturday it was mid-morning when Gianfranco strolled in. Casually dressed in beige trousers and shirt, with a lambswool sweater draped across his broad shoulders, he looked sensational.

'Ready to go, Kelly?' Gianfranco asked in a deep, husky drawl.

'Yes.' She rose to her feet; something warm quivered deep down inside her as her eyes collided with deep dark brown. 'Though I don't know about this dress,' she said, suddenly nervous. It was one Judy had brought in for her, a mint-green wild-silk sheath buttoned down the front from the slightly scooped neck to the hem. Good for feeding, Judy had said. But to Kelly it seemed a little short and a lot clingy under Gianfranco's discerning gaze.

In one lithe stride he was beside her and, wrapping an arm around her waist, he smiled down into her exquisite face. 'You look perfect,' he murmured, and kissed her.

Excitement lanced through her nerve-endings, and sent her pulse-rate racing. Kelly was shocked, fighting against a tide of fierce physical awareness. She had just had a baby; somehow she had thought it would make a difference but it didn't.

'Come on, the car, the baby carriage—everything awaits you, Kelly, and I have a surprise for you.' Gianfranco slashed her a gleaming smile and kissed her again.

'But first the nurse has to carry the baby off the premises and I have to sign you out.'

They stopped at the reception desk, and Kelly waited impatiently while Gianfranco completed the paperwork. She glanced across, as he seemed to be taking a long time. When he came back to her his smile had gone and he looked oddly sombre.

'Something wrong?' she asked, fearful that she might not be able to leave yet.

A muscle jerked beside his unsmiling mouth. 'No, nothing at all.'

But, by the time the car drew up outside the Casa Maldini, though Kelly had tried to hang on to her optimism, she'd failed. They had hardly spoken a word, and it was a tight-mouthed, austere Gianfranco who helped her into the house with baby Anna.

Their reception committee was waiting. Carmela, Olivia and the staff—everyone fussed over the baby. Until Gianfranco took the carrycot holding the baby in one hand and Kelly by the arm with the other. 'I'll take you upstairs.'

A few minutes later Kelly was standing in the middle of a nursery, with every conceivable object a baby could possibly want or need. Gianfranco, with amazing efficiency, had placed the sleeping child in the delicate crib provided, and, straightening up, he gestured with one elegant hand to one of two doors set in one wall. 'Through there is a connecting bedroom with *en suite* bathroom for the nanny, and another bathroom.'

'It is beautiful.' She gazed around at the walls, skilfully painted with a nursery-rhyme scene of a rolling landscape with all kinds of field animals. When her eyes finally reached the figure in the mural she realised it was Little Miss Muffet. She bit back an exclamation at the sight of the enormous spider! She was lost for words...

'While you thought the guest rooms were being decorated this nursery suite was being devised, and it connects with ours. It was Olivia's idea to keep it a surprise.'

The spider should have told her Olivia had had a hand in it, she thought cynically. 'Yes, it is a lovely surprise.' Tearing her eyes from his, she moved to the cot and smiled down at her sleeping baby. 'We will be fine here, won't we, darling?' she murmured.

Straightening up, she glanced back at Gianfranco. 'I think I'll check out the rest later; I could do with a lie-down.' She tried to smile brightly, but it didn't quite come off as she crossed to the door that connected with her old room.

Long, elegant fingers wrapped around her arm and stopped her. 'Wait, Kelly; Mamma has arranged some interviews this afternoon to choose a nanny—obviously you will want to take part,' he said, scrutinising her with dark, impassive eyes.

'No,' she said tightly. 'Let's get one thing clear right now: I am not having my baby looked after by a nanny for quite some time—if ever.' On this point she was adamant. 'Is that clear enough for you?'

'Yes, clear enough. I get the message. I can't do anything right in your eyes.' Gianfranco suddenly exploded. 'Why didn't you tell me it was your birthday last Saturday?' His abrupt change of subject made Kelly's head spin. 'I would never have known except when I signed you out at the hospital the nurse suggested if you had given birth an hour earlier you and Anna would have shared the same birthday. Have you any idea how low that makes me feel?'

'Not half as low as I felt,' Kelly responded with muted sarcasm.

'I don't need to be reminded of that.' Dark hooded eyes met hers. 'Do you imagine for one second I would have left you alone on your birthday, or that I don't regret missing the birth of our child?'

'If you say so,' she agreed. Their baby was sleeping not three feet away and she did not want to argue. She heard his hissed intake of breath and put a hand on his arm. 'I'm sorry but I assumed you knew it was my birthday when you applied for our marriage licence. And you took my passport.' She justified her reasoning, but, seeing the grim expression in his eyes, she changed tack. 'I know you are a Leo, born on the third of August,' she tried to placate him. 'But perhaps it is a male-female thing—Venus, Mars. Let's not fight about it.'

'You're right; I should have known. I'll make it up to you.' He reached out, his strong hands clasping her tense shoulders, drawing her closer. He dropped a kiss on her upturned face, his dark eyes burning into hers. 'I don't deserve you.'

Her heartbeat thudded and she drew in a quick, excited breath, a wealth of emotions welling up within her. She loved her husband, the father of her child; what else mattered? Kelly lifted her hands and circled his neck, pushing her fingers slowly into his thick, luxuriant hair, and she had an almost unbearable longing to be held in his arms again, to feel the long length of his hard body pressed against her without the inconvenience of her once swollen stomach. 'No, you don't, but you've got me,' she teased.

He didn't laugh, but bent his head and let his tongue dart between her parted lips in an erotic invasion that turned her bones to water, and made her tremble. 'Ah, Kelly,' Gianfranco husked in his accented drawl. 'You don't know what you do to me.'

She knew what she would like to do to him, she thought breathlessly, the hardness of his aroused body setting her imagination in overdrive.

'Oops, sorry.' Olivia giggled. 'I couldn't wait to find out what Kelly thinks of the nursery.'

Gianfranco's arms fell from around Kelly. 'She loves it. Don't you, *cara*?'

The phrase 'dropped like a hot brick' sprang to mind... Kelly moved stiffly back and, glancing at Olivia, said, 'Yes, it's great.'

Anna started to cry. Saved by the baby. 'If you will excuse me, Anna needs feeding.' Crossing to the cot, she lifted Anna in her arms.

'You really should get her on a bottle as soon as possible,' Olivia offered. 'Then anyone could feed her.'

Ignoring the other woman's comment, Kelly settled down on the nursing chair, and in minutes Anna was suckling greedily at her breast.

Gianfranco surveyed the mother and child, his black eyes fixed on Kelly's breast. Astonishingly he felt a stab of something very like jealousy towards his daughter. He wanted to be where Anna was, and his body warned him to get out fast. 'I must go,' he said shortly.

Kelly glanced up, but he was already exiting the room. Now that she was left with the baby and only her thoughts, the events of the last half-hour ran through her mind, and warning bells rang loud in her head. What kind of woman had she become? Placating Gianfranco at any cost! Actually apologising to him for his forgetting her birthday! Afraid to speak her mind except on the simplest of topics, in case she offended him or his family. What kind of weak example of womanhood was that to set her precious daughter?

Four weeks later, restless and unable to sleep, Kelly slid out of bed. She glanced briefly at the connecting door to the room Gianfranco occupied and for a moment was

tempted to go to him. But he had decreed no sleeping together until she got the all-clear from the doctor at six
weeks. He had given her a diamond necklace to match the
bracelet as a belated birthday present, also a car for her
personal use, and he was good with Anna—when he was
around. But he was not around much.

Love was a fearsome emotion, she thought with a sudden
shiver. Except for the love of her child—*that* was totally
different. She would do anything for Anna, and with that
thought in mind she walked along to the nursery. Her breast
milk was drying up, and the nurse had suggested supple-
menting Anna with formula, but the baby did not seem to
like it much. Quietly she opened the nursery door, and
shock held her rigid for a second.

Olivia had Anna in her arms and was feeding her with
a bottle of formula. 'What the hell do you think you are
doing?'

Olivia looked at Kelly. 'Practising for when you are
gone.'

Snatching the baby from Olivia's arms, Kelly was shaking with anger. Now she knew why Anna was not feeding
well from her. 'Get out, and keep away from my child,'
she snapped.

'Your child?' Olivia sneered. 'Haven't you realised yet?
Gianfranco is going to dump you as soon as you stop
breast-feeding and we are going to be a family. Why do
you think your so-called marriage was only a civil cere-
mony in England? He does not even need to divorce you
to marry me in church, you stupid cow.' And Olivia walked
out.

Kelly tried to tell herself it was the ravings of a slightly
unhinged woman. But deep inside she didn't really believe
it. She had put up with a lot to stay with Gianfranco, but
when it came to her daughter she would fight like a tigress.

CHAPTER NINE

Three years later.

ST AIDEN'S COVE in Cornwall was virtually deserted, although it was early summer. Kelly stood beside the outcrop of rocks on the tiny beach and watched her daughter methodically shovelling sand into a small red bucket; nothing would stop Annalou's determination to build a sandcastle, and Kelly was vividly reminded of Gianfranco. Annalou had her father's eyes, and also his confidence. Nothing seemed to bother her.

Unfortunately the same could not be said for her mother, Kelly conceded wryly. It had been a June day, much like this, when she had made her escape from the Casa Maldini.

In the end it had been quite simple, she recalled, her mind going back to that traumatic time. She had told Gianfranco what Olivia had done, and he had told her she was overreacting. They had argued, but for once Kelly had refused to give in.

The night before she was to go to the doctor for her final check Gianfranco had walked into her bedroom. She could see him now in her mind's eye, looking breathtakingly handsome, wearing only a robe, his long tanned legs slightly splayed as he had stared down at where she lay in the big bed. 'Tomorrow you see the doctor—I am right?'

His dark eyes, smouldering with a brooding intensity, had caught and held hers, and she had felt every nerve in her body leap to quivering life. As if compelled to, he had

132

sat down on the side of the bed and taken her in his arms. The warm, musky male fragrance had been dizzyingly familiar as he'd covered her mouth with his and kissed her with a hungry, urgent passion.

'Bella mia,' he had groaned against her mouth, his supple fingers stroking her breast, his other hand lifting to sweep the soft fall of her hair down her back, his night-black eyes skimming her upturned face, the softly parted lips. 'Hurry back tomorrow. I am dying of frustration.' He'd kissed her again.

Fool that she was, two kisses had been all it took to convince her that her fears were groundless and Gianfranco loved her. They were a family, and the future looked rosy. But his parting comment—'Remember to ask the doctor to give you the Pill—it is the safest birth control'—had dented her euphoria somewhat.

But nothing like the shock she had got the next day. She had returned from the doctor's, excitement bubbling inside her, and headed straight for Gianfranco's study, unable to wait to give him the good news.

Even now it still hurt, Kelly thought bitterly. The door had been partially open, and she had seen them together. Gianfranco and Olivia in each other's arms. Judy's warning, Olivia's actions—all had made perfect sense. But it was what her husband and Olivia had said that had horrified her, had prompted her decision to leave immediately.

'I can assure you, Olivia, Kelly and I will certainly not be having any more children.'

'So why wait? Get rid of her now, Gianfranco. I can take care of Anna Louise; I love her.'

No way was Olivia getting her hands on Kelly's child.

Kelly had acted her socks off. Her sad face had been genuine when she'd told Gianfranco later that the doctor had said another week, but not for the reason he had thought. With a little persuasion Gianfranco had agreed Kelly and the baby could visit Judy Bertoni for a few days, while he took the opportunity to clear up some business in New York.

Ironically Gianfranco had provided her means of escape. He had given her a state-of-the-art mobile phone, with instructions to call him any time, so that way he would not disturb her when she was busy with Anna Louise. Raiding his study, she had looked for her passport and by a bizarre stroke of luck she had seen the new one Gianfranco had obtained for her with the baby listed on it. He had said he would take her on holiday, but she couldn't believe the nerve of the man. Obviously the holiday was to have been her pay-off! Well, he was in for a rude awakening, she had vowed.

The next day she had been on a plane to England, and by the evening she had emptied her bank account—the money from the sale of her house a welcome bonus. She'd made a point of telephoning Gianfranco several times, so as not to arouse suspicion. The final call she had made the next morning, when she'd left the hotel where she had spent the night. She told him she had left the car at Rome Airport and she had left him. Olivia was welcome to him, but not her baby.

He had still been yelling down the telephone when she'd switched it off and thrown it into the road. A black cab had put paid to it.

Remembering her honorary Uncle Tom from her childhood, she had headed for his home in Cornwall, and he had welcomed her and Anna Louise with open arms. After he had heard her story, he had insisted she stay with him in his cottage overlooking the bay. He had introduced her to his neighbours as Kelly Hope, his recently widowed niece, and her baby, and told Kelly all she had to do to stay hidden was to stay off any government computer—Inland Revenue, health and education systems etc.

With the money from her house in Tom's bank account, it had been no problem. Ellen Jones, whose father was a friend of Tom's, ran a small gymnastics club in the nearby town of Newquay, and she had given Kelly a part-time job helping out at the club, and she paid her cash.

For three years Kelly's life had worked fine. She glanced back at Annalou. She was gritting her little teeth, her whole attention concentrated on making the 'biggest sand castle ever' for Uncle Tom.

Kelly's eyes squeezed shut in a spasm of pain. They had buried Tom yesterday. It was Tom who had shortened Anna Louise to Annalou. Yet they would never, ever see him again. She would never hear that deep Cornish burr in his tone as he comforted and cajoled her. Their lives would have to change…

Gianfranco hesitated, to control the pounding of the blood in his veins. It was Kelly, more beautiful than ever, her luscious body honed to perfection; even the cheap black dress she was wearing could not hide that. The neckline was low enough to reveal the upper curve of her breasts, and short enough to reveal her shapely legs. Her silver-blonde hair was longer, untamed, falling almost to her waist. He had given her everything, and she had betrayed him…

Silently he moved forward.

'So this is where you are hiding, Kelly?'

After three years Kelly recognised the deep, accented voice instantly. Her eyes flew open, shock lancing through her. She stared; she couldn't help it. He was standing not a foot away. An all-powerful male. His tanned face had a few more lines, but they only added to his dark, devastating good looks. He was dressed in perfectly tailored black trousers and a black roll-neck sweater. With his great height and broad-shouldered, virile body, that simply oozed sex appeal, he looked like some avenging angel—or devil—she realised as his eyes, black as night, roamed over her with unconcealed contempt. Goosebumps erupted all over her body and she reeled back against the rock as though blasted by the banked-down violence in his eyes.

'You,' she murmured—it was as if by thinking about him earlier she had conjured him up. Quickly she tore her gaze away from his and sought Annalou, who was sitting in the sand, her brown eyes turned quizzically up at the man.

'Big man,' Annalou said. 'Do you want to make a sand-castle?'

Gianfranco glanced down, and immediately dropped to his haunches with lithe grace. 'Anna, isn't it?' he said softly. And as Kelly watched the transformation on his hard, sculptured face was miraculous. He smiled at the child. 'I love to make sandcastles, Anna.' He reached out a none too steady hand to touch the fiery red hair surrounding the angelic-looking face. Two sets of identical deep brown eyes met and fused with each other. It was instant attraction.

Kelly saw Annalou grin, and she had to swallow the lump in her throat that threatened to choke her.

'My name is Anna Louise Hope, but everyone calls me Annalou,' she corrected him seriously.

Gianfranco shot a glance at Kelly that would have blistered paint. But the face he turned back to the child was gentle. 'Then I shall call you Annalou,' he said with a smile. 'And you can call me Daddy.'

Go straight for the jugular, why don't you? Kelly was struck dumb by Gianfranco's blunt admission.

Annalou looked up at Gianfranco with wide excited eyes.

'You my daddy?' she began...then, glancing up at Kelly, 'Mummy?' she said. Only one word, suddenly unsure for the first time in her young life.

Narrowed black eyes lifted to Kelly. Gianfranco was watching her like a great black panther waiting to pounce. He scanned her ashen face and horrified eyes. 'Tell her, Kelly,' he drawled silkily.

Kelly could hardly string two coherent thoughts together, let alone a sentence, she was shivering in so much shock. Annalou hadn't noticed the absence of a daddy in her life until she had started playschool after Easter. Kelly had told her he lived far away, and left it at that. Looking down at the man and the child, at the triumph on the face of the former, she realised with a sinking heart she had nowhere to go... She was trapped.

Bending her knees, she dropped in the sand beside Annalou. 'Yes, sweetheart.' She instinctively curved a protective arm around her shoulders. 'This—' She saw the derision in Gianfranco's eyes, and stammered helplessly. 'He—I mean, this man is your daddy.'

Annalou wriggled from under Kelly's arm and threw herself at Gianfranco. 'You really are my daddy.' And with childish logic added, 'Uncle Tom had to go to heaven, so he has sent you.'

Gianfranco closed his arms around Annalou, and held her hard to his broad chest. 'Something like that.' Gianfranco slashed a look of utter hatred over the top of the child's head at Kelly, and, leaping smoothly to his feet with Annalou still in his arms, he added, 'But, unlike your Uncle Tom, I am going to stay with you forever.' He made his promise softly, with a kiss on the child's smooth cheek that Annalou happily returned.

Lifting his proud head, his narrowed eyes studied Kelly's stricken white face with a kind of grim satisfaction. 'Isn't that so, Mummy?' He demanded her compliance, the derision in the deep, dark drawl obvious to Kelly, but lost on the child.

Kelly staggered unsteadily to her feet; she had turned even paler as the full horror of what he had said sank in. She had escaped Gianfranco once, but he would never make the same mistake again. At least not where his child was concerned. As for her… She was probably just as dispensable now as she had been three years ago.

'Mummy?' Annalou's small face was turned towards her, her expression expectant, waiting for her mother's confirmation of the wonderful news.

Suddenly, Kelly was overwhelmed with the most horrible feeling of guilt, mixed with a deep-rooted fear for the future. But she could do nothing but agree…

Hours later, the sandcastle built and marvelled over, Kelly had been unable to avoid taking Gianfranco back to her home. Tom had left her the house in his will, along with his money—which was actually what was left of hers! He had lived on his pension, and it had stopped at his death. Kelly had been worrying over what she was going to do, but now that worry was replaced with a much greater fear. Annalou was too young to notice, but Gianfranco had made it obvious by each look and gesture in Kelly's direction that he was biding his time until they were alone, and then all hell would break loose.

'Read a story, Daddy,' Annalou said, now bathed and safely tucked up in bed. She turned away from where Kelly stood to Gianfranco, at the opposite side of the bed. 'Please.'

Kelly felt a swift stab of jealousy at how quickly her daughter had fallen under Gianfranco's spell. But then she glanced across at him, his black hair dishevelled, his dark eyes smiling down at the little girl. Kelly doubted any female from three to ninety-three could resist his seemingly effortless charm. He was lounging on the bed, one arm around Annalou, the other holding the book, one long leg stretched out on top of the coverlet, his other foot on the floor. The fabric pulled taut across his muscled thighs was enough to make any woman groan, and to Kelly's dismay she was no exception...

Her hands turned into tight fists at her sides. She had to get out of here; the tension that had simmered between Gianfranco and her all afternoon was driving her mad and her nerves were at screaming pitch. 'Goodnight, sweet-heart.' She leant over and pressed a kiss to the downy cheek, making sure to avoid any contact with Gianfranco, and, straightening up, she added, 'I'll leave Daddy to tuck you in.'

She almost ran out of the bedroom and stumbled back down the stairs. Walking into the kitchen, she eyed the table, a grim smile curving her lips. They had eaten beans on toast for dinner—hardly Gianfranco's style, but Annalou's favourite. Quickly she set about cleaning up. She washed the dishes, wiped down the benches—anything to keep busy so she did not have to think. But she could not control her thoughts so easily. Finally, with nothing left to do, she wandered back into the living area and across to the picture window that filled almost the whole wall. She stood still as a statue and gazed out over the sand and sea.

She had been so happy—perhaps not happy, she amended, but certainly content here. It had been an old barn, converted quite simply with the front door at one end opening into one large living area, and a kitchen, utility room and rear door at the back. A staircase up the side of the wall led to a galleried landing with two bedrooms and a bathroom. It stood on its own on the outskirts of the small fishing village, and had originally been rented out as a holiday home. Tom had stayed here once and then bought it.

Tom; if only he were here now, she thought as she squeezed back a stray tear. He would know what to do. He would know how to handle Gianfranco. Still, straightening her shoulders, she drew in a deep breath. She had matured a lot in the last three years; she was no longer the naïve pregnant girl who had jumped at Gianfranco's offer of marriage, flattered that he had hired a detective to find her.

'Quite a spectacular hiding place,' a deep husky voice drawled mockingly behind her, and she jumped as if she had been shot, as she had not heard him come downstairs.

Spinning around, she faced him. 'How did you find me?' Kelly went straight onto the attack. 'Detectives again,' she sneered.

Gianfranco studied her with half-closed eyes. 'Your friend Tom wrote and told me.'

Of all the things he could have said, that was the most hurtful; every vestige of colour drained from Kelly's face as she looked up at him with wide, pain-filled eyes. 'No. No, I don't believe you.' Tom would never have betrayed her trust.

He shrugged his broad shoulders. 'Please yourself.' Strolling across the room, he sank down on the leather sofa, his long legs stretched out before him in nonchalant ease. 'It is immaterial now. Though I must congratulate you on doing a very good job. At first I thought it might be postnatal depression, and I checked with Dr Credo. But no... You had left his surgery one hundred per cent fit and happy, with six months' supply of contraception pills in your hand,' he said drily.

Colour flared in Kelly's cheeks, her lie revealed. She threw Gianfranco a sharp look, deeply disturbed at his tone, but she could read nothing from his coldly remote expression.

'You are a great actress. I take my hat off to you,' he said with cutting cynicism. 'I spent a fortune hiring the best detectives known, and they could find no trace of you after you left a London hotel. You have remarkably little family—a second cousin on your father's side in Bristol, I believe, was as near as they got. Your mother was brought up in an orphanage. You were incredibly lucky—or it was great planning?—to have met Tom, my dear wife.' His mouth twisted chillingly. 'Or you would never have got away with it.'

Uneasily Kelly listened and frowned. Gianfranco was right in every detail about her escape, and her family, so why would he lie about Tom telling him where she was? Horrified, she knew Gianfranco was telling the truth. Suddenly her legs felt wobbly, and she moved to sit down in the nearest armchair. She couldn't take it in. Tom had betrayed her. Kelly glanced warily across at Gianfranco. 'When did he write to you?' she asked quietly.

'Ten days ago, from his hospital bed apparently. But I only received the letter last night. He knew he was going to die, so he wrote to inform me that, although he loved you as his own, he could no longer take care of you.' He said it so dispassionately that Kelly was lulled into a false sense of security. In a way she could understand Tom's reasoning, even though she wished with all her heart he had not done it.

'He also said it was time I took care of my own.' One dark brow arched sardonically. '"Chance would be a fine thing," I believe, is the English expression.'

Lounging back on the sofa, Gianfranco was an incredibly attractive vision of relaxed masculinity. To her horror, despite being in the midst of fear, Kelly felt the familiar flood of sensual awareness heat her whole body. He was still the same insensitive, arrogant devil, she reminded herself firmly. 'Yes, well, now you have the chance. You made sure of that when you blurted out you were Annalou's father,' she declared bitterly. 'You could have traumatised the child,' she added for good measure.

In a blur of movement Gianfranco lunged off the sofa and hauled her to her feet by her upper arms. The transformation was incredible; his face was so taut with rage that Kelly feared for her safety.

'You dare say that to me, you bitch! You, who deprived her of her father for three years.' His night-black eyes, leaping with violence, bored into hers. 'Deprived me of my child. Replaced me with your lover, Tom.'

'No. No,' Kelly cried, stunned by his reasoning. 'Let go of me.' She tried to shrug his hands off, terrified at the fury in his tone. 'It wasn't like that.'

She tried again to pull free, but his hands tightened on her arms. 'Yes, it was, my beautiful, traitorous wife. Don't take me for a fool—this house has just two bedrooms,' he said through clenched teeth, and hauled her closer into his hard body.

'There are two beds; I share with Annalou.'

'For appearances' sake, I don't doubt,' he snarled. 'And tonight I share with Anna Louise. *Dio*, you even deprived my child of her family name, and I—I, her father—had to hear her tell me she is always called Annalou.' He focused on her with a dark, blistering anger that heightened the tension to breaking point. 'I saw you today on the beach and I wanted to kill you. Three years of hell you have put me through. But you are not worth losing my freedom for. Instead I am going to make sure you suffer as I have,' he hissed with lethal intent.

The fear and tension that had held her since the moment

he had walked back into her life finally snapped and Kelly exploded. 'Make *me* suffer! You did that from the day you married me. You never wanted me, all you ever wanted was my child. You never even tried to get in touch with me until you discovered I was pregnant. And even—'

'You stood me up,' Gianfranco cut in ruthlessly. 'I do not run after any woman.'

Kelly sucked in air convulsively. He was the same arrogant, conceited jerk he had always been. 'Exactly,' she ground out mockingly. 'As I said, it was only my baby you wanted. Amazing the lengths you would go to, even marrying me for that manic Olivia you love so much. You kept me in that great mausoleum of a house like a damned broodmare; you never believed a word I said, but Olivia or your mother could do no wrong.'

One hand slid upwards to curve around her jaw, and as he tilted her head back his glittering eyes bored down into hers. 'You dare to blame *me*?' he raked back scathingly. 'I gave you everything a woman could want, and you repaid me by running off with my child.'

'You gave me everything but your support.' Everything but your love, she almost added, but stopped herself in time.

'You had that, and if you had demanded more I would have given it. But, no, shall I tell you why you ran?' He emitted a harsh, cynical laugh. 'Because in your usual childish fashion you listened to rumour and innuendo and jumped to a whole lot of false conclusions. I told you I had never loved Olivia as anything but a sister in poor health and needing help, but you chose not to believe me.' His fingers tightened almost cruelly on her chin and she tried to jerk her head away.

'Look at me,' he demanded savagely, and she did, suddenly aware of the brush of his thighs against her own, the close proximity of his large body. 'I might have made mistakes as a husband, but I never deserved what you inflicted on me, the loss of my child.'

Maybe not, Kelly conceded—she had felt guilt over the years, but above all she knew he was lying. She had seen him with Olivia in his arms, and heard him.

He looked at her, and subtly the atmosphere changed. He was smiling, his hard eyes glinting with a devilish light as he said silkily, 'But you know what really gets me? I have tortured myself for three years, wondering if you were all right, staring at the one photograph of my daughter on her first birthday that you deigned to send me. Posted in London with no way to trace it.' He traced his fingers smoothly over her cheek while his other hand closed firmly around her waist. 'Clever, very clever. Then I discover you have a lover—"Uncle" Tom,' he spat, in a voice laced with bitter contempt.

'No.' She saw it too late in his darkening eyes. Felt it in the hard length of his body pressed against her. 'No, Gianfranco,' she cried, but his mouth took hers and she was shamed by the incredible hunger that shook her to the depths of her being. *No*, her mind cried as her lips helplessly parted to his savage invasion.

Held against the hard length of his body, she tried to struggle, but the total contact was like an electric shock to her system, awakening a dormant awareness she could no longer control.

'Three years you owe me,' he grated as his mouth moved down her throat, then her shoulder.

'No.' Kelly shuddered as his hand slipped inside the bodice of her dress to cup her breast, and at his touch desire swept through her, leaping from nerve-end to nerve-end with a speed that shocked her as it seduced her. The scent of him filled her nostrils, and the taste of him—ah! The familiar taste of him as once more his mouth covered hers was like a drug to her sensually deprived body.

She knew she should stop him, but at that moment his fingers rolled across her rigid nipples and she was swamped in a wave of heat. Instead her arms slipped around his neck. He lowered her to the floor, his lips against her throat, her shoulder, his long body stretched out half over her, his knee between her thighs.

Gianfranco stared down at her; her dress was around her waist, and a scrap of white lace was the only barrier to the heated centre of her. He slipped the dress down her arms and bent his head, his mouth suckling on a rigid nipple.

Kelly shut her eyes, a low moan of dismay and desire equally mixed escaping her. She felt his hand slide up her thigh, his long fingers slip beneath the lace barrier and wrench it from her body. His hand curved around the blonde curls at the apex of her thighs, his long fingers intimately exploring the velvet flesh. She was hot and damp and she shook with a need, a want so agonisingly painful that she cried out his name. And from that moment on she was lost in her own fevered response to the awesome passion he evoked in her body, which had been celibate for far too long.

Rearing up, Gianfranco touched the tip of his tongue to the tip of each breast as he deftly unfastened his trousers. Then he slid his hands under her and lifted her up to accept the fierce thrust of his manhood, burying himself deep in the hot, tight heart of her femininity.

There was nothing tender or gentle about their coupling. More a wild white-water ride, two bodies grinding, drowning in a savage, primitive hunger, hand and mouth, tooth and nail, they caressed and clung until Kelly's body convulsed first, in an agony of exquisite pleasure, and Gianfranco followed, his great body shaking with the force of his release. For a long moment he lay with his face buried in the soft curve of her throat and shoulder, then with a violent curse in Italian he rolled off her.

Kelly understood the curse he had uttered, and heard the slight sound of his clothes being readjusted, the zing of a zip. She shivered. Not with cold but with shame.

Leaping to his feet, Gianfranco ran a hand through his rumpled hair. Damn it, that was not supposed to have happened. He stared down at her, his black eyes raking over her flushed face and the abandoned position of her slender body, and he grimaced. But she was so hot and willing she couldn't help herself. Once she had been all his. *Dio*, how many more men had tasted her sweetness? he wondered grimly.

Kelly saw her briefs lying on the floor and silently groaned, shame keeping her from looking at Gianfranco.

'You could earn a fortune as a porn star. Straighten yourself up, for God's sake,' Gianfranco said bluntly, his voice as hard and cold as ice.

Ashen-faced, Kelly pulled up the bodice of her dress, pulled down the skirt, picked up the torn briefs and, ignoring him, walked into the kitchen and shoved them in the bin.

Zombie-like, she crossed to the bench, filled the kettle at the tap, and switched it on. She took a cup from the shelf and spooned instant coffee into the cup. With her hands propped on the bench and her head bent she waited for the kettle to boil. And all the while her mind was screaming. What have I done? She couldn't believe she had surrendered to Gianfranco so quickly, so uninhibitedly. Three years, she silently groaned, and as far as her traitorous body was concerned it could have been yesterday. Nothing had changed.

Yes, yes, it had, Kelly amended and, straightening up,

she lifted the kettle and poured the water into the cup. She had changed…she was a much stronger woman; bringing a child up on her own had taught her a lot. She lifted the cup of black coffee to her lips with a slightly trembling hand, and after the first mouthful she felt marginally better. At least she had wiped the taste of Gianfranco from her mouth. If only she could wipe him from her life so easily, she thought bitterly.

'Good idea. Make one for me,' Gianfranco commanded.

Kelly spun around at the sound of his voice, about to tell him to make it himself, but caution stopped her. She had a much bigger argument to win than who should make the coffee. He was sitting on one of the three seats at the small breakfast table, his dark head turned towards her, his hooded gaze completely unreadable.

She cleared her suddenly dry throat. 'Black with one sugar, is it?'

Gianfranco raised an eyebrow. 'You remembered.'

'Some things are hard to forget,' she muttered, turning back to the bench and taking another cup from the shelf. And she wasn't talking about the coffee. One look at him looking so cool and composed, while she was still reeling from the shock of having just made love—No, not love, sex—annoyed her immensely.

'Yes, it is gratifying to know I can still make you burn, and cry out *my name*,' he emphasised in his deep, husky drawl. 'It makes the future so much easier; a celibate marriage never appealed to me.'

Kelly realised in stricken apprehension that Gianfranco had read her mind. She could not speak; her tongue was glued to the dry roof of her mouth as she fought to remain calm. She poured water into the cup with her heart hammering in her chest. No way was she resuming married life with Gianfranco, as his words implied.

'From what I have seen, Annalou seems to be a happy, well-balanced little girl.'

Kelly inwardly sighed with relief at the change of subject, but her relief was short-lived. She turned to look at him, and the gleam of mocking triumph in his black eyes sent a shiver down her spine. 'Yes, she is,' Kelly said curtly, and moved to place the cup of coffee on the table in front of him. 'And she is very happy here. She has lots of friends.' If she could convince him to give her a divorce, Kelly thought, nervously chewing her lip, she wouldn't mind his having some custody rights.

'This place looks like a holiday home. I understand you now own it.' He lifted the cup to his mouth and swallowed the hot coffee, then he added smoothly, 'I suppose Annalou can still spend the odd holiday here and keep in touch with her friends.'

'Odd holiday!' Kelly exclaimed. 'We live here.'

'Not any more—we are leaving for Italy in the morning.'

It was no more than she had expected from the moment she had set eyes on him on the beach, but it was still a terrible shock. Kelly staggered back to lean against the kitchen bench, not trusting her legs to support her. 'No, Annalou and I are staying here.' She had to stay in control, be convincing, but she was trembling inside. 'But I am prepared to be reasonable. You and I can get a quickie divorce, and we can share custody. You can visit whenever you like.'

'Have you finished?' he demanded with eyes as cold as the Arctic wastes, and for a moment her mind went blank. 'Good. Because I am taking my daughter back to Italy. Any visiting to be done will be at my discretion.'

'You can't do that. I won't let you.' Kelly burst into speech, trying to sound firm, but nothing could disguise the slight tremor in her voice. The full enormity of what he

had said hit her like a punch to the stomach. She felt sick
with fear, and she knew she was fighting for her daughter's
well-being, never mind her own. 'There is no way I will
allow Annalou anywhere near Olivia without me.'

'So, come with her.'

'No.' She instinctively denied the possibility. 'And you
can't take Annalou without my permission.' She said it, but
didn't really believe it. She knew very well that Gianfranco
was a man who got exactly what he wanted. Kelly doubted
anyone had thwarted him in his life except herself. If she
was honest she was slightly amazed she had got away from
him for so long. It was there in the proud tilt of his head,
the dark, mocking eyes watching her like an insect under
the microscope.

'With you in jail I will have no problem.'

'Jail!' What on earth was he talking about?

Gianfranco set his cup down and the clash when it hit
the saucer indicated he was nowhere near as calm as he
appeared. He stood up, his mouth curving in a cruel smile.
'I had Kelly Hope checked out the minute I read the letter.
A man was waiting at Exeter Airport when I arrived today
with the details. You are a respected widow with a child,
who for the past three years has been working for an Ellen
Jones who owns a gym. Correct?'

At the mention of her job, Kelly suddenly saw where he
was leading. 'My private life, where I work, is no concern
of yours,' she snapped back.

'Perhaps not, but I wonder what the Inland Revenue will
make of you working—the black economy, I believe is the
British term for it, or cash in hand?' He chuckled without
humour. 'Tax evasion is a serious offence, punishable by a
term of imprisonment in some cases.'

Stunned, Kelly could only stare at him. He met her gaze
with sardonic challenge as he continued. 'I would not worry

too much—it would be your first offence.' He gave a very Latin shrug of his broad shoulders. 'Of course, poor Ellen Jones will also be in trouble. Then there is the kindly doctor, a friend of Tom's, who, without any formal identification from you, has privately taken care of your health, immunised my daughter. He also will suffer.'

Kelly jerked upright and took a step towards him, rigid with fury, her eyes flashing blue flames. 'You are despicable!' she cried. 'You would hurt innocent people, my friends, just to get back at me?' She shook her head in utter disbelief. Jail was no idle threat.

'I don't have to,' he injected as she stared at him in outrage and shock. 'It is your decision, Kelly. You can come with Annalou and me to Italy, or stay here and face the consequences.' He looked at her with triumphant amusement in the black depths of his eyes. 'Either way, I get my daughter.'

CHAPTER TEN

IT HAD been no choice at all, Kelly thought, staring down at her sleeping daughter for a long moment before lifting her head and eyeing the huge painted spider still on the wall with distaste.

Even if she'd faced up to the Inland Revenue, though she had done wrong, she doubted she would have ended up in jail. She had never earned enough money to pay tax anyway. At least that was what Tom had told her. But it would have meant betraying Ellen and probably the doctor. The deciding factor, the one thing Kelly had not been able to countenance, had been to allow Annalou to visit Italy without her, and be subject to Olivia's poisonous presence.

Kelly turned quickly as Gianfranco's voice broke into her musings.

'She is a beautiful child.' He was standing at the opposite side of the bed, his huge body stooped to press a kiss on Annalou's cheek, and the sheer size and strength of him, along with his state of undress, sent her pulse-rate rocketing.

He was wearing a navy-blue towelling robe, loosely belted at the waist and ending mid-thigh, his toned olive skin and mat of black body hair exposed between the low lapels of the garment. Kelly flushed at where her thoughts were leading and looked away, tension in every line of her slim body.

Despising her weakness at reacting so instantly to his unexpected appearance, she was curt in her response. 'Yes, she is, and I want her to stay that way, without any influence from your sister-in-law.' She masked her frustration and fear by prompting coldly, 'I suppose Olivia will be joining us for dinner?'

They had arrived at the Casa Maldini at four. Much to Kelly's surprise, her mother-in-law, Carmela, had welcomed her with open arms, and apologised for not being more of a friend to her the last time she had lived at the house. And Anna was still here, engaged and getting married in August.

Annalou had loved the house immediately, unlike her mother not in the least intimidated by the vast building and the servants. By the time Kelly, with the help of Anna, had put the little girl to bed, Annalou in her usual determined fashion had secured a promise she could be a bridesmaid at the wedding. The only person Kelly had not seen yet was Olivia.

Strolling around the bottom of the bed, Gianfranco stopped beside Kelly and glanced down at her with dark, enigmatic eyes. 'Olivia will not be joining us for dinner, or any other meal. She does not live here any more.'

'What? But you said last night—' And she stopped. He had neither confirmed nor denied Olivia's presence; he had simply said, 'So, come with her.' Kelly searched his face but she could read nothing from his bland expression. 'You let me think...'

One dark brow arched sardonically. 'What you wanted to think, *cara*.' He drawled the endearment. 'I wanted my wife and daughter back in my home, and I used any and every means at my disposal. In my book marriage is for life. Remember that and we will get along fine.'

'Olivia left? When?' Kelly still had trouble believing it, though she had no trouble believing the rest of her indomitable husband's statement. He was a ruthless devil when it came to getting his own way.

'A few weeks after you. She is now married to a banker and living in Switzerland.'

Was he broken-hearted at losing Olivia? Lowering her head to hide her astonishment at his revelation, she surreptitiously glanced up at him from beneath the screen of thick lashes. He didn't look it. In fact, Kelly suddenly noted that his dark eyes were blatantly roaming over her slender body in studied masculine appraisal. She had already bathed and dressed for dinner in a violet satin slip dress with spaghetti straps supporting the bodice, and to her shame she felt her breasts harden against the soft fabric in tingling arousal. She dropped her gaze, but that was worse. Last night he had taken her without even removing his clothes, but tonight, with his robe gaping open, she realised she had never seen so much prime male naked flesh in three long years...which did nothing for her temperature, or her temper.

'Oh, for God's sake, go and put some clothes on!' she exclaimed, brushing past him and heading for the door. 'Dinner is at nine.' Damn! She sounded like his mother, and his husky chuckle did nothing to calm her quivering nerves.

Kelly barely touched the food, even though she had hardly eaten anything all day. She'd phoned Ellen to ask her to keep an eye on the house. Then they'd flown from Exeter by private plane to Verona, and the final leg had been the car journey to the Casa Maldini. Everything had happened so fast, she couldn't think straight; she felt positively light-headed.

A brief glance at Gianfranco seated at the head of the table and Kelly turned an apologetic smile to Carmela and stood up. 'It has been a long day, and I am rather tired, so if you will excuse me I think I will go to bed.'

'Of course,' Carmela responded, 'I understand.'

'You have had a traumatic week. You need a rest,' Gianfranco said smoothly. 'Sleep well.'

He'd got that right, she thought as she stifled a yawn. Tom's death, the funeral five days later, and Gianfranco the next day—it suddenly hit her she had barely slept or eaten for a week. The fact Gianfranco had recognised it was surprising; he wasn't known for his sensitivity.

'Goodnight,' she said firmly, but she could not meet his dark watchful eyes, and she speedily crossed the room with more haste than grace.

Kelly glanced around the bedroom, it was the same room she had occupied before, and Anna had laid her cotton nightie out on the massive four-poster bed. She wondered if Gianfranco still occupied the bedroom next door, and immediately dismissed the thought. Contemplating Gianfranco in bed, any bed, did nothing for her peace of mind.

Picking up her nightie, she walked into the adjoining bathroom. In minutes she had had a shower, and, after drying herself quickly with a large bath towel, she slipped the nightie over her head. A brief glance in the mirror and she grimaced. The white nightie was a simple mass of gathered cotton falling from a round neckline to her feet—with her hair brushed loose and her face free of make-up, the only point of colour was the purple rings under her eyes. She looked like a ghost.

Shrugging her shoulders, Kelly returned to the bedroom, and then on to the nursery. She stood for a few minutes staring down at her sleeping daughter, and then made a silent prayer that Annalou would be happy here. For herself she didn't care. Annalou was everything.

Had she done the right thing? A resigned sigh escaped her. Deep in her heart Kelly knew she had never really had a choice. Gianfranco turning up yesterday had only precipitated matters, as if she was honest Kelly had already decided to get in touch with Gianfranco after Annalou had asked about her father at Easter. Tom's illness and the need to look after him had given her an excuse to delay, but with Tom's death she'd had no more excuses. Which was probably why she imagined she had conjured Gianfranco up yesterday on the beach, she thought wryly.

Sighing, she touched a finger to her daughter's cheek. Had she jumped to conclusions three years ago, as Gianfranco had said? If not, did it matter that Gianfranco had loved Olivia? Olivia was no longer in the equation.

For years she'd tried not to think about her husband because it had hurt too much, but now she faced the facts. Last night had taught her she was still as deeply attracted to him as ever. Only now she did not call it love. She was older and wiser, and for the first time since meeting Gianfranco again Kelly considered the possibility of trying to make the marriage work.

She didn't trust him, but then again he didn't trust her, so they were equal on that score. But they did have a child together, and she did not doubt his love for Annalou; in the short twenty-four hours the bond between father and daughter was obvious for all to see. If Kelly wanted to keep her daughter and give her the happy home life she deserved— and she did—then maybe the best way of achieving that was to reconcile with Gianfranco. Quietly closing the door behind her, Kelly walked back to the bedroom. She was too bone-deep tired to make a decision now, and, crawling into bed, she curled up in a foetal position, yawned widely and within seconds exhaustion claimed her.

Kelly's lashes fluttered against her cheeks and her head fell onto the pillow, the supporting warmth removed. She frowned; she could hear voices and instinctively curled her legs across smooth flesh, unwilling to wake up yet. She snuggled deeper, against a hard male thigh—aroused male! Her eyes flew open and she jerked up. 'What the hell!' she exclaimed, her head spinning: the other side of the bed was occupied.

'*Buongiorno, signora.*' Anna was in the process of placing a tray with coffee and two cups on the bedside table.

Gianfranco was in her bed, lounging back against the pillows, looking incredibly sexy and, if Kelly wasn't mistaken, stark naked. She tore her eyes away from Gianfranco and back to Anna, and quickly moved to the edge of the bed. 'Thank you for the coffee, but where is Annalou?' she demanded.

'Run along, Anna,' Gianfranco instructed. 'I will explain.'

He had a hell of a lot of explaining to do. Like why was he in her bed? Kelly thought furiously, her blue eyes flashing back to his.

'Relax. I am informed our daughter is washed and dressed, and at this moment in the kitchen having breakfast. She's apparently completely besotted with the household cat,' he drawled. His deep voice, husky with sleep, was like a caress across her skin, and his slumbrous dark eyes were holding her own.

Her whole body flushed with heat, she swallowed convulsively, and tore her eyes away from his as she recalled the feel of his hard thighs only moments ago. Dynamic and all male, he projected a raw virility that was almost frightening in its intensity. Her gaze lingered over the black hair on his broad chest angling down to where the fine sheet covered his thighs. Surely he had not looked so good years ago.

She gulped and said the first thing that came into her

head. 'Why did Anna bring your coffee—it always used to be Aldo?'

A cynical smile quirked the corners of his firm lips. 'It occurred to me I was perhaps a little insensitive three years ago when you were a new bride, and sharing a bed with a man for the first time, to have another man wake you up in the morning. I was used to Aldo but I remember you used to blush and huddle under the bedclothes.'

'You're right, I did.' For a moment she was touched that he had recognised her embarrassment, even if it was three years too late.

'Of course it hardly matters now,' Gianfranco drawled, reclining back against the pillows. 'But I had already arranged it before I left for England and discovered the life you had been leading.'

Kelly recognised the sarcasm, and any softening she had felt towards him vanished in a puff of smoke. 'It was a hell of a lot better than the one I had here,' she gibed, and slid off the bed before turning to challenge him. 'And now perhaps you can explain what you think you are doing in my bed.'

'*Our* bed, Kelly.'

'That's rich coming from you. You couldn't get out of it fast enough when we were married,' she shot back with some sarcasm of her own. It still rankled, even after three years.

'As I recall, you never objected —the safety of our unborn baby was your top priority.' He looked at her quizzically, as if she had just given him the answer he had been looking for. 'I did not know you cared.'

'I didn't.' She shook her head, her long hair flying around her shoulders in tumbling disarray. 'I don't.' He was far too astute and she was mortified at what she had almost given away. 'I'll pour the coffee before it gets cold,' she mumbled, and made a production of filling the two cups while fighting to regain her self-control. Taking a deep breath, Kelly turned back to face him and held out the cup and saucer.

He took it from her hand and drank, replacing the cup on the bedside table; then, leaning back, he watched her with an impassive expression that made Kelly very nervous, and when he spoke in a voice lacking all emotion she almost spilled her own coffee.

'The last time you were here we spent a few weeks sharing a bed, and then the doctor said no sex. I slept in a separate bedroom because I wanted you with a hunger, a passion I could not control.'

Kelly sucked in a breath, her startled gaze flying to his, and she saw the heat in the glittering black depths of his eyes he did not try to hide, and felt reciprocal warmth ignite low in her belly.

'Yes, Kelly. I was a danger to our unborn child because I did not trust myself not to make love to you. You only had to touch me, smile, and everything else faded into oblivion against the irresistible urge to have you.'

Her mouth fell open in amazement. As excuses went it was a Lulu, but she wasn't sure she believed him. She bit her lip. 'Yes, well,' she muttered, and, lifting her coffee-cup, she drained it. The conversation was becoming far too personal, and she didn't want to go there...

He stretched out, the long, powerful length of him at ease, but his hooded eyes were watchful on her. 'You know it's true,' he drawled. 'You proved it on one memorable occasion when you gave me the relief I craved, but afterwards I felt guilty, less of a man because I could not do the same for you at the time. But now there are no such restrictions and, if the other night is anything to go by, you are desperate. You obviously want me as badly as I want you.'

Kelly clenched her teeth and slammed her cup down on the table. She would not rise to his bait, she vowed, and counted to ten under her breath.

'No denial. Very sensible,' Gianfranco prompted, and at that she did swing back to face him.

'I suppose you are now going to try and tell me you loved me all along and not Olivia?' she sneered.

His mouth twisted in a mockery of a smile. 'No, I am not. You never trusted me before. Why should now be any different? As for love—it does not come into it.' His expression hardened. 'The first time we made love or had sex…whatever, you drove me crazy, and you still do. This time we will share a bed, and we will enjoy each other until such time as the passion fades. It will be fun with no consequences.'

He laughed without humour, his dark eyes sardonically appraising her stiffly held figure in the childish white nightgown, her long hair falling down her back in a tumbling mass. 'You may look like an innocent but we both know you are an experienced lady now. How many have there been besides Tom?'

Kelly's hands clenched into fists, anger rising like a tidal wave. 'Why, you…'

'No, don't answer that.' He held up a large hand. 'We will not talk of the past—it is enough Tom is dead,' he reminded her brutally. 'And you and I are very much alive.'

Her eyes met his and she flinched at the implacable intent she saw in them. 'You can't be serious.'

'Never more so, *mia cara*.' Gianfranco's mocking voice echoed in the tense silence. He swung his long legs off the bed and stood up, totally unconcerned at his nudity.

It wasn't fair, Kelly thought helplessly, that the sight of

his naked body could arouse her, and she was shamed at her weakness. She didn't hesitate. She ran for the bathroom and locked the door behind her, her heart pounding like a jackhammer in her breast.

It was half an hour later before she ventured out of the bathroom; showered and wearing a white towelling robe, she peered anxiously around the bedroom, but it was empty. In a matter of minutes Kelly was dressed in a blue cotton summer dress, and with sandals on her feet went looking for her daughter.

The sight that met her eyes as she descended the stairs brought a reluctant smile to her lips. Gianfranco was on all fours and Annalou was straddling his back, her tiny hands knotted in his hair, yelling, 'Faster, faster, Daddy.'

As Kelly reached the bottom step Gianfranco stopped at her feet and lifted his head. 'Get her off me before she tears every hair from my head. I'm begging you on my knees.'

He quite literally was, and Kelly laughed and lifted Annalou off her father's back and onto her feet. 'What's all this about?' She tried to sound serious but the light in her eyes gave her away.

'Daddy said he would buy me a pony, and I was practising. He is going to take me riding some time.'

It was obvious Annalou was completely at ease with her daddy and her new home. Kelly bent down and gave her a quick hug, and, straightening up, wistfully wished she could feel as comfortable in Gianfranco's presence. He had risen to his feet, and, casually dressed in cream cotton trousers and a white shirt, he took her breath away.

'I promised to take Annalou out for the day to buy her a pony.'

'What? A pony?' Kelly said, pulling her thoughts back from the wayward track they were heading. 'To ride, you mean?'

Gianfranco's grin slashed across his face. 'Yes, a pony and yes, to ride,' he said blandly. 'You had better come with us, to make sure you approve of the purchase. I thought we could make a day of it and have lunch in Verona. Perhaps buy some summer clothes for you both.'

'Please, Mummy, yes.' Annalou pulled at her skirt.

Kelly cast a fulminating look at Gianfranco. So their clothes were not good enough and he was going to spoil the child rotten. But her voice was steady as she said, 'If you can spare the time that would be nice.' She wasn't going to argue in front of Annalou.

Taking Kelly by the arm, he said softly, 'I have a lot of time to make up, and we both know why.'

His lean, elegant fingers, lightly restraining her arm, heated her skin. The threat inherent in his comment silenced Kelly. A narrowed glance up into his darkly handsome face told her she had no choice, and, grasping Annalou with her free hand, she allowed herself to be ushered out of the house.

He took them to stables on the outskirts of Verona. And to Kelly's amazement the owner actually had a tiny Shetland pony. Annalou was delighted, but took a fit of the sulks when her father explained the pony could not go with them, but had to be transported later by horsebox. The little girl soon brightened when they arrived in Verona. After buying a host of toys and clothes, Gianfranco suggested a drive to Lake Garda and the hunting lodge, with its small private beach.

Kelly's mouth went dry as he took off his shirt and sat down beside her, his eyes fixed on Annalou paddling around in the shallows. Kelly looked away from his bronzed torso rippling with muscle and swallowed hard. It brought back the disturbing memory of the last time she'd been here with Gianni, when she'd been innocent and in love. Sure she'd been loved in return, she had felt free to touch him, caress him.

Suddenly she was blinded by tears, and was thankful for the sunglasses that hid her eyes. Kelly blinked and stared sightlessly out over the lake, hating to admit it, but knowing it was true: whether he was commoner or count, betrayer or betrayed by her desertion, she still felt the same. She ached for him with the same agony of need, the same hunger, and the same love...

They had been married and lived together for six short months and slept together for little more than one. Perhaps this time it would be better—at least there was no Olivia...

Alarmed at where her thoughts were leading her—straight back into his bed—she said quickly, 'Time to go; it's getting late, and Annalou has had enough excitement for one day.'

Gianfranco nodded his head, and she saw the amusement lurking in his dark eyes. As though he had read her mind and understood exactly how she felt.

'Too many memories, *cara*.' Rising to his feet, he slanted her a heavy-lidded look. 'But now we make new ones.' And, striding across to Annalou, he picked her up in his arms. Kelly had the unenviable feeling she wished it was her.

It had been a lovely day, Kelly agreed with Annalou as she tucked her into bed. But, going down for dinner half an hour later, she was a bundle of nerves. She sat through the meal, making polite conversation with her husband and her mother-in-law, but underneath her emotions were in turmoil.

She heaved a sigh of relief when after the coffee stage Gianfranco said he had some paperwork to attend to and left.

Kelly's relief turned to panic a couple of hours later when, walking out of the bathroom wrapped in only a bath towel, she stopped dead. Gianfranco was standing by the bed wearing a towelling robe. A bottle of champagne stood on the nearby table with two glasses.

'A toast to our reunion,' he drawled mockingly, and as she watched he opened the champagne and filled the two glasses, and then walked towards her with a glass in each hand. He held one out to her.

Her heart thumped erratically; it was a moment of truth, Kelly knew. If she took the glass and said nothing she was agreeing to resume being his wife in every sense. She lifted her head, her wary blue eyes scanning his harshly set features, and fleetingly the thought crossed Kelly's mind that he was not quite as confident as he appeared. Quickly she dismissed the idea as wishful thinking. The decision was hers to take...true. But realistically she knew Gianfranco would have his way whatever...

She took it. 'Thank you, I could use a drink.' The slight quiver in her voice revealed her apprehension.

His brilliant dark eyes roamed over her with explicit sexual hunger, and then met and held hers. Suddenly the atmosphere crackled with electric tension.

Kelly felt her body heat as he raised the glass to his mouth. 'To my wife, the mother of my child; our marriage starts here.' And he drank it down in one gulp.

With a hand that trembled, Kelly lifted her glass to her lips and took one long swallow. Then spluttered and lowered her head as the bubbles went down the wrong way.

Gianfranco took the glass from her hand and moved to put them both on the bedside table. Then he turned back to face Kelly. 'Come here,' he commanded tautly.

She lifted her head. Her watering eyes collided with his smouldering dark gaze, and instantly she was swamped by her intense awareness of him. His sinfully sensuous mouth, the proud tilt of his dark head, his lithe, powerful physique poised and waiting...

Mesmerised by his male beauty, Kelly took a step forward and another... She felt her face flush, heaviness in her breasts, her nipples hardening. She hesitated and swallowed hard, before slowly moving forward again. He wasn't going to make this easy for her...

'You look nervous,' he drawled softly. His hands reached out to her tense shoulders and drew her closer, his dark eyes black and knowing on her lovely face. 'Yet there is no need; you are an experienced woman,' Gianfranco said thickly, one hand curving around her throat and tilting her head back.

If only he knew he was the only man who had ever touched her, Kelly thought, but didn't tell him. She had to keep some defence, even if false, she thought as she trembled with need as all her senses heightened to fever pitch.

His hand slid down over her breastbone, caught the towel, and with one deft movement she was standing naked before him. Tiny flames glinted in the black eyes that slowly ravished her shapely body with a long look, before his head bent and his mouth brushed surprisingly gently over hers until he felt her willing response, then his tongue delved sensually into the moist interior of her mouth.

'Exquisite,' Gianfranco groaned against her lips, and tipped her back onto the bed. For a moment eyes as dark as jet raked over her, then he shrugged off his robe.

It was what Kelly had been waiting for. Naked and powerful, he was sheer masculine perfection. Her blue eyes greedily surveyed his great body, the harsh glare of the artificial light gleamed on muscle and sinew, and she ached for him with a hunger so deep that she could not wait. She reached out her hand.

'Soon, *cara*.' He smiled in purely masculine promise as he came down to her and immediately ravished her mouth with his again.

Not another word was spoken over the next few hours. It was an erotic banquet of the senses.

Kelly had never experienced such an intensity of sensations as Gianfranco extorted from her, nor felt the incredible need to do the same to him. Finally, when he was buried deep inside her for the third time, her heart pounding, lost to everything but the explosive excitement she craved, she gazed wildly at him. She saw the skin pulled taut across his cheekbones and the savage satisfaction as he watched her shuddering on the painfully exquisite edge of release. Then with every thrusting stroke he drove her quivering body to a climax so intense she cried out in ecstasy, mindless to everything but the wonder of his total possession.

Wrapped in his arms, exhausted but fulfilled, she should have stayed silent, but she didn't...

CHAPTER ELEVEN

GIANFRANCO rolled off the bed and headed for the bathroom again. Kelly groaned; her body aching but satiated, she lay on her back and waited for his return. Her dreamy blue eyes followed him as he walked back, lithe and naked, to sit down on the side of the wildly rumpled bed.

'You will run out of those before long,' she teased. It was a new experience for Kelly to have him wear a condom, though he had quickly taught her how to put them on. 'I don't know why you bother.' She lifted her hand and stroked gently up his chest, her heart full of love.

'Because, Kelly,' Gianfranco's dark eyes gleamed down with grim amusement into her own, 'much as I want you, I am taking no chances with my health. The Pill protects only against pregnancy, not sexually transmitted diseases. I don't know where you or Tom have been in the past three years,' he drawled hardly.

As the import of his words sank in, Kelly stared at him, incapable of tearing her gaze away from his handsome but suddenly cynical features. Her hand fell from his chest, her fingers curling into fists at her sides. The last few hours meant nothing to him, nothing at all. She had been in danger of fooling herself yet again.

She lowered her lashes to hide the pain and fury in her eyes, and choked back the surge of anger constricting her throat. She wasn't on the Pill—the supercilious swine had just assumed she was, and on top of that he thought she might be diseased. If ever the veil of love was torn from a woman's eyes, it was in that moment for Kelly.

She could explain, maybe even convince him, but she was damned if she would. With a superhuman effort of will Kelly forced a smile to her love-swollen lips. 'Whatever you say.' Forcing a wide yawn, she turned away from him and pulled the coverlet over her shoulder. She felt the mattress depress as he lay down beside her, and she made no resistance when he wrapped an arm around her and pulled her into the warmth of his body. What was the point? She loved him, wanted him, but some small part of her heart froze. That night set the pattern for the weeks ahead.

The next morning Gianfranco introduced her to the nanny he'd employed to help her look after their daughter, a large widow in her forties, Signora Mussi. He also made it plain the woman was a guard against any repeat of Kelly's desire to run away with Annalou. The rest of the staff had the same instructions. Kelly didn't bother to object because she knew it would be useless, and in any case she intended to stay with her daughter whatever the cost.

In the weeks that followed Kelly's life fell into a routine. She spent all day with Annalou, in the evenings and weekends Gianfranco joined them, and the nights... The nights were spent with her husband.

Kelly had studied chemistry, but nothing had prepared her for the sexual chemistry between them. Every night in the huge four-poster bed they came together with a hunger, a need that knew no bounds. Gianfranco taught her every subtle erotic nuance the human body was capable of and then some! And she was a willing learner. They tormented and teased and pleasured each other, and afterwards fell into a sleep of utter exhaustion in each other's arms.

Before, when they had been together, Kelly had been pregnant the whole time. Their lovemaking had been wonderful, but now she realised just how restrained Gianfranco had been. Three years later he had no such inhibitions; he delighted in her body with a fervour that bordered on obsession. Sometimes in the early morning she would wake to find him watching her with an intensity that was scary. He could spend hours caressing every inch of her body. But it was the same for her. She gloried in the freedom to explore his hard masculine frame, until finally they would find yet more ways to please each other.

At first Kelly was hopeful the passion they shared would bring them closer together, but as the weeks moved into months she had to accept it would not.

In day-to-day life they were Mummy and Daddy, for Annalou. They obeyed the social niceties on the few occasions they appeared as a couple, at business dinners or events at the Casa Maldini. But the rest of the time they were like two strangers. Gianfranco was as much a workaholic as ever, but without travelling abroad. Kelly busied herself with Annalou and making friends with the staff and, much to her surprise, Carmela. Lunches and shopping trips were quite frequent occurrences and went some way to combating Kelly's sense of loneliness.

It was a glorious, hot, sunny day on the twenty-third of August, Anna's wedding-day. Annalou was standing in the entrance to the small village church, a picture in a froth of pale blue silk with cream roses embroidered around the Peter Pan collar, and the crinoline skirt caught up in scallops around the bottom with cream satin bows.

'Now do as the chief bridesmaid tells you and stand still and behave yourself,' Kelly told her quietly. 'Your daddy and I must take our seats.'

'Yes, Mummy.'

Sitting in the front pew, Kelly glanced around the church. She recognised most of the faces: they were all people who worked for her husband. She cast a sidelong glance at

Gianfranco beside her. The expertly tailored silver-grey silk suit he wore fitted his impressive frame to perfection, but could not hide the raw animal magnetism of the man. She studied his dark, devastatingly handsome face, and surprisingly discerned tiredness around his eyes and mouth that gave a harshness to his features. He glanced back at her as though sensing her surveillance, one perfect ebony brow arching quizzically.

Kelly shook her head and stared straight ahead. So he looked a bit haggard—not surprising, the way he worked—and played. The last two nights they had made love with a desperation on Kelly's part she was not proud of. Still, they did not have the kind of relationship that allowed her to show concern for him. Anyway, she had enough problems of her own. The biggest one having arisen two days ago—when she had collected Annalou's dress from Verona she had also visited Dr Credo, and discovered she was pregnant again. At first she had been delighted, until she'd remembered Gianfranco's telling Olivia he wanted no more children.

The bride was beautiful, the service, the photos, the reception...everything was perfect, but Kelly went through the whole thing worried sick.

'It was the bestest wedding ever,' Annalou said later that evening, standing in the nursery, washed and ready for bed, having finally been persuaded to take off her bridesmaid's dress. 'Anna was beautiful; my wedding will be like that. Was yours, Mummy?'

Kelly chuckled. 'Something like that,' and, glancing across at Gianfranco, she was surprised to see what looked like a flicker of pain in his dark eyes. He had just been laughing and telling Annalou she was a little princess.

'Into bed.' Kelly watched as Annalou climbed on the

bed, and then, bending over her, she tucked her in and kissed her.

'You looked lovely as well, Mummy,' Annalou murmured sleepily. Kelly swallowed the lump in her throat, touched by her child's words.

'Thank you, sweetheart. Now go to sleep.' Straightening up, she smoothed her hands down her hips, straightening the skirt of her dress. It was a designer gown in heavy silk, French navy trimmed with cream, with a low-cut square neck that revealed the slight curve of her breasts, and short sleeves. It followed the line of her shapely body to perfection. But not for much longer, she thought wryly.

'I don't think I told you how beautiful you looked today.' Gianfranco's husky drawl impinged on her musings, and suddenly he was beside her, his hand on her arm. 'My daughter reminded me.'

'You don't look so bad yourself,' Kelly murmured, her gaze resting lightly on his large, lithe body as he led her from the room.

'Thank you.' Gianfranco grinned. 'But I think our little princess took the prize, don't you?'

'Yes. Of course,' Kelly agreed and glanced speculatively up at him as they entered the sitting room of their suite. The wedding and Annalou seemed to have put him in a good mood, but then he usually was relaxed around Annalou. Maybe this was her chance to do some fishing and find out how he really felt about another child.

'She is growing up fast,' Kelly ventured, sinking down onto the sofa and kicking off her shoes; her heart was racing but she battled to remain cool.

'Yes, she is a darling child, and she looked a picture in that dress,' Gianfranco responded, walking across to the bar and pouring a good measure of whisky into a crystal glass. 'Want one?' He raised his glass.

Kelly shook her head. 'No,' and for a second wondered what he would say if she just came out with it. *Sorry, I can't—I'm pregnant.* But she wasn't prepared to take the chance. Instead she continued, 'But I sometimes wonder if maybe Annalou is a bit lonely with only adults for company,' she suggested. 'Maybe we should consider having another child—a brother or a sister for her.' She waited with bated breath for his response.

Gianfranco almost choked on the whisky and, draining the glass, he put it down, his dark brows drawing together in a frown. Had she taken leave of her senses? He crossed to where she sat, looking perfectly relaxed, and stared down at her. A tentative smile played around her luscious mouth, but her gorgeous eyes were oddly serious. He knew what she was like for leaping into things. Her latest idea had to be nipped in the bud immediately.

'No. Annalou is perfectly happy, and she has friends at pre-school. Another child is out of the question,' he told her bluntly. A nerve ticked in Gianfranco's temple, and he laid his hand on her shoulder, kneading her collarbone to emphasise the point. 'Forget it, Kelly. I don't want any more children.'

She trembled at the warmth of his hand on her flesh, but her blue eyes locked onto the implacable darkness of Gianfranco's and she had her answer. He was deadly serious and it hurt like hell. Deep down inside she had nursed the hope that perhaps her Italian had not been so good three years ago, that she had misinterpreted what Gianfranco had said. Now that hope was gone.

'Tough,' she said, shrugging off his hand and rising to her feet. 'Because I'm already pregnant.' She didn't wait to hear his response, but headed for the door.

'No—no.' Gianfranco grabbed her arm and whirled her

around to face him. 'Tell me it isn't true,' he demanded through clenched teeth.

His fingers bit into the flesh of her arm and a surge of anger coloured Kelly's cheeks, but she forced herself to remain calm; this was their unborn child they were discussing and anger would get them nowhere. 'It's true; get used to it,' she snapped, and watched as he closed his eyes for a moment. Perhaps now it was a *fait accompli* he might like the idea. But any hopes in that direction were squashed once and for all when he opened his eyes.

His face hardened into an impenetrable mask. 'Has the pregnancy been confirmed by a doctor?' he demanded, and his cold, clipped voice chilled her to the bone.

'Dr Credo. Two days ago.'

'Is it mine?'

A harsh, humourless laugh escaped her. That was the one question she had not expected, but she should have done, given he thought she had slept with Tom and was too dodgy to touch without a condom. 'Oh, yes. I am nine weeks pregnant—work it out for yourself. History repeating itself,' she drawled with bitter sarcasm. 'The tumble on the floor in Cornwall.'

His black eyes narrowed to mere slits in the harshness of his face. 'You were on the Pill.'

'No. You *said* I was on the Pill, because you told me to take it three years ago and Dr Credo told you I had done so,' Kelly said sweetly, but inside she was raging. Her husband, Count Gianfranco Maldini, was a very wealthy, very powerful man, one of an almost extinct breed of dinosaurs that believed once they had demanded a course of action it would be pursued *ad infinitum*. The conceit was colossal.

Gianfranco's dark eyes grazed over her slender but voluptuous body, and fear such as he had never imagined possible was staring him in the face. He frowned down at her. 'No matter, Kelly. Much as it goes against my belief, in this case it is not too late. A termination is in order.'

She shivered, closing her eyes against the pain. He had it all cut and dried.

'I will have a word with Dr Credo.' He was still talking, and Kelly saw red.

Her fingers curled into fists and her free hand swung though the air. She punched him straight on the nose. 'Take that, you no-good scum of the earth,' she yelled; it had hurt her hand but it was worth it, as Gianfranco reeled back, letting go of her arm in the process.

'I have had enough of you to last me a bloody lifetime.'

They hadn't spent as much as a year together as man and wife, and in that time Kelly had suffered every emotion known to man and then some, all because of Gianfranco. But his latest betrayal was the worst, the absolute pits. She glared at him with wild eyes; he had straightened up and was holding his nose, blood seeping through his elegant fingers. Serves the bastard right, she thought furiously. And all the hurt, the anger she had kept in check for so long, came spewing out.

'All you ever wanted from me was sex, from the first time we met. I was never good enough to be your wife or the mother of your child. You would never have married me, except you found out I was pregnant and your precious flaming Olivia wanted a baby. The pair of you decided to have mine. Olivia told me herself: the civil marriage in England meant nothing, but was just a means to get my baby. You could still marry her in church.'

She didn't hear Gianfranco's horrified, '*Dio, no.*' Her fury, unleashed, flowed like vitriol over his proud head.

'I saw you both in the study when I came back from the doctor's, wrapped in each other's arms. And you—you...' she shrieked. 'Telling her that we would certainly *not* have any more children. Caressing her while she said she loved *my baby* and would take care of her.'

Kelly didn't notice Gianfranco's sudden stiffening, his dark eyes fixed intently on her furious red face as he listened to her wild outburst while she was too bound up in her own emotional blood-letting…

'Well, I am glad I foiled the pair of you, and I am glad Olivia left you. My only regret is that you found me again. You don't deserve a daughter like Annalou. And to think I actually thought I loved you.' Kelly shook her head, her blonde hair falling from its precarious chignon to tumble around her shoulders. 'Even today I tried to convince myself—perhaps I had not understood the Italian language so well, maybe you had not said what I thought. More fool me!' Tears blinded her eyes. 'You soon put me right; I must have been mad.'

Kelly had never felt such complete and utter desolation in her life. But she squared her shoulders, steely determination in every line of her slender body. Her moist blue eyes glistened in her drawn face as she looked up at Gianfranco. 'Murder my baby, would you?' she grated in a raw voice. 'Over my dead body.'

His head jerked back as though she had punched him again, and every vestige of colour fled his hard face, leaving him looking grey and haggard, and his sensuous mouth was a taut, cruel line as he said through his clenched teeth one word, *'Exactly.'*

To have him admit everything she had feared was true with one word was like a knife skewering her heart. All the blood drained from her face and she drew a deep, unsteady breath, her blue eyes curiously blank. 'The truth at last.' Unconsciously rubbing her sore knuckles, she added in a voice devoid of all emotion, 'I will see you in hell before I let you near me again.' His large hand reached out to her and she batted it away. 'Don't touch me. Don't you dare touch me.'

His strong features were torn by some intolerable emotion. 'No, Kelly, no, you've got it wrong.' And before she could move he hauled her hard against his long body, his dark gaze moving over her anguished face. 'I know about your mother.'

Through the mist of her despair she looked into his eyes, and the anguish she saw there more than matched her own. 'My mother—you know she and Tom were lovers?' Why on earth was he harking back to what was ancient history?

'No, I didn't know that,' he said in a toneless voice. 'But I do know she died in childbirth, and the same could happen to you. When I said *exactly*, I was responding quite literally to your comment ''over my dead body''. Don't you see?'

She stared at him in complete confusion, then slowly, through the utter despair enfolding her, Kelly felt the first glimmer of something like hope. The pain, the passion as his dark gaze swept over her, was plain to see. He was worried about *her*, and she was so astonished she made no demur when he lowered her down onto the sofa and sat beside her.

'If I have to choose between you and another child...' He didn't look at her as he began to speak, his head bent, his hands clasped between his spread knees, the knuckles white with strain. 'I don't care if I condemn my immortal soul to hell. It has to be you. I can't bear to lose you again.'

Stunned blue eyes widening as the import of his words sank in, Kelly turned towards him and placed a hand on his arm. 'You're frightened?' she whispered.

He nodded and, sitting up, his head lifting to look at her, he gave her a somber, almost angry glance. 'Terrified,' he admitted, and Kelly instinctively knew his anger was not directed against her, but himself.

He agitatedly ran his fingers through his hair before continuing. 'The day I saw you in the hospital bed after giving birth to Annalou Dr Credo told me you had haemorrhaged, and then he told me your mother died in childbirth, but you didn't like to talk about it. But...'

He hesitated for so long Kelly thought he couldn't finish. 'So?' she prompted.

'In that moment, when I realised you could have died having my child when I wasn't even there, I recognised something I had never really thought existed: I love you quite desperately.'

'So you didn't love me when we married,' she murmured sadly to herself, but Gianfranco heard.

'I didn't know what love was,' Gianfranco said urgently and, grasping her slender shoulders, he made her face him. 'You want the truth?' His dark eyes blazed with a determined light. 'You shall have it. I met you, a bright, beautiful girl, and I wanted you. Then, because of a stupid masquerade about my name, I lost you. In my pride, my arrogance, I vowed I would not chase after you when you stood me up. So I did not. I saw other women, but it was no good, I suffered torment through months of celibacy.' He glanced at her. 'It had never happened to me before.'

Kelly amazed herself by smiling at his arrogance. 'Poor you.' But his words gave her the first glimmer of hope.

'Yes, well.' He grimaced with a wry twist of his lips. 'Even when I discovered you were pregnant and searched for you I still never thought of marriage. But the minute I saw you again I heard myself proposing marriage. I was as astounded as you were then; I justified it by telling myself it was the sensible thing to do. My mother was hinting I should marry and provide an heir, so why not?'

'I don't think I want to know this,' Kelly cut in

'You wanted the truth and you are getting it,' Gianfranco prompted bluntly, his mouth twisted and hard. 'It crossed my mind you might be a gold-digger, and Olivia certainly thought so, but I didn't care. Perhaps I loved you then but could not admit it, or didn't need to...' he offered with unconscious masculine conceit. 'All I knew was that I wanted you and the baby. I moved you into my home and my bed, and my life went on much the same as before.'

He shrugged as though he was ashamed of his lack of insight. 'I can remember wondering why my married male friends complained about the confines of married life. I felt no such constraint. I did not alter my lifestyle one iota, and I had the added bonus of having you in my bed at night. Then you complained about Olivia and I was hit by divided loyalties.'

'Was she your lover?' Kelly asked painfully. He had said he loved her, but not until after she had given birth to Annalou, and she did not know how that made her feel.

'No, never.' His hands tightened on her shoulders. 'You have to understand about Olivia. I was sailing with Alfredo the day of the accident. He died and I was saved, and I have carried the guilt with me ever since. I always thought it should have been the other way around.'

Her response was a long sigh. 'Oh, no.'

'Yes,' he admitted, his expression bleak. 'With hindsight I know I over-compensated. I dismissed your fears about Olivia because of my own feelings of guilt and because, if I am honest, it made for an easier life to blame your hormones. Hell, what did I know about pregnant women? When I should have supported you I failed miserably. I put up with more from that woman than you can imagine. But the last day, when you said you saw us in each other's arms plotting against you, I swear on our daughter's life it was not like that.'

Kelly drew in a sharp breath—to vow on Annalou's life, he had to be telling the truth. 'Then what *was* it like?' Kelly pressed him. She needed to know before she could let the tiny flame of hope in her heart blaze free.

'She knew you had gone to the doctor's, she knew I was planning to take you on holiday, and she flung herself at me ranting about how much she loved me, and when we could marry. I was horrified—I had never, ever thought of her in that way. It was then I finally realised she was very ill. I tried to calm her down, but she declared we would have to wait until you produced a boy before we could marry. I guess what you saw was me restraining her by the arms, after having told her she was talking rubbish and I was certainly having no more children.'

Kelly opened her mouth to speak, but Gianfranco went on in a harsh voice, 'She was back in the mental hospital two weeks after you left. She recovered, and the man she's married is a widower with three children. She got what she wanted. But it was too late for me; because of my own blind insensitivity and pride I had lost you and our child. Which brings me back to the present.' As if compelled, he bent his dark head and kissed her, hard and brief, before rearing back slightly, a dull red flush staining his high cheekbones. 'I love you too much, Kelly,' he grated in a tortured voice. 'I cannot let you take the risk of having another child. I couldn't live without you.'

She stared at him, and what she saw in his dark eyes, the love, the torment, made her heart expand in her chest until she thought it would burst with incredulous joy. There was no doubting his sincerity: Gianfranco did love her.

Suddenly the world was a marvellous place to Kelly, and

hope and happiness surged through her. Blue eyes glowing, she said, 'I love you too, but you are crazy, Gianfranco.'

'Crazy!' he exclaimed and, pulling her onto his lap, he added, 'Crazy in love. But as your husband I have to protect you from yourself,' he said seriously. 'No more children.'

Kelly curled up on his lap and linked one arm around his broad shoulders. She knew he needed to be convinced his very real fear was groundless. 'You can't stop me.' She lifted her finger and put it over his lips for a moment as he would have objected. 'And you're wrong; there is no risk, or none that every pregnant woman in the world does not face.' Her hand dropped from his face and she grasped his arm to emphasise her point. 'I am not my mother—she died from complications and, to be blunt, because, although she was forty-two and considered at risk, she insisted on having the child at home. The baby was delivered with the cord around his neck, dead. The midwife did her best, but when my mother haemorrhaged it was another two hours before she made it to the hospital.'

'Your father must have been mad to let her stay at home,' Gianfranco commented in typical autocratic macho fashion.

'That was exactly what Tom said.' Kelly felt the tension in his broad frame at the mention of Tom. 'Tom was a lifelong friend of my mother's—they were in the orphanage together, and were lovers in their youth. Tom went to sea, and when he came back my mother had married my dad. Tom was like an uncle to me, a friend of the family; he appeared now and then with hosts of gifts. But after my mother's death he had a furious fight with my father—he blamed him for Mum's death—and we never saw him again. But I always had his address.'

A dawning realisation made Gianfranco's dark eyes gleam with relief. 'No wonder my detective could not find you. No relation, and no contact since you were a child.' He shook his dark head and looked down into her lovely face, wrapping his arm more firmly around her waist, pressing her closer to the warmth of his body. 'You took a big chance searching him out,' he said seriously, an oddly speculative expression in his black eyes. 'He could have been an axe-murderer, anything.'

'You really are a worrier,' Kelly teased with a grin. 'Anyway, I knew no one else,' she said simply. 'And you haven't needed to use protection, because he was never my lover,' she added for good measure. It still hurt that Gianfranco had assumed the worst about her. 'I never had a lover, which is just as well, the speed at which I seem to get pregnant,' she added with dry humour.

His incredible dark eyes closed for a moment, and then he opened them and his voice was hard, quivering with emotion he no longer tried to hide. *'Dio grazie.'*

'Tom was a good man; he loved Annalou and I, and I miss him,' Kelly said softly.

Gianfranco drew in a deep breath and looked into her expressive sapphire eyes. He was going to tell her the truth, to exonerate his own behaviour, but the sadness he saw stopped him. His investigators had discovered Tom had never been a sailor, but he had travelled abroad—and spent quite a lot of time in jail for fraud. Gianfranco knew what went on in some jails, and he had genuinely feared for Kelly's health. The relief of knowing she had never slept with the man, or any other, was overwhelming, and he smiled gently down into her beautiful face. It was no wonder Tom had been able to keep Kelly hidden so successfully. The guy had been a master of the art.

He put his hand under her chin and tilted her face up. 'I'm sure he was, Kelly. He kept you and Annalou safe and he gave you both back to me. For that I will always be grateful.'

He brought his head down to cover her mouth with his own. She felt the rapid thumping of his heart against her breast as he eased her against him and her lips parted willingly, warmly, to the thrusting demand of his tongue. He kissed her with a hungry, desperate need until, lifting his head slightly, his lips moved against her smooth cheek. 'I loved you and longed for you for three years; I still do, and always will, Kelly.' His words vibrated against her skin, and echoed to her heart's core.

Kelly looked deep into his eyes, searching for the truth, and she shivered at the raw emotion she saw there. 'And the baby?' she had to ask.

He jerked his head back and looked straight at her. 'We will have the best medical care on the planet, and if it is a boy we will call him Tom.'

She laughed, her blue eyes sparkling with humour, and, reaching up, she wrapped her other arm around his neck. 'You don't have to go that far,' she teased, her fingers tangling in the dark silk of his hair, pulling his head back down towards hers. 'I rather like Gianni, after the first and only man I have ever loved or ever will love,' she confessed, and she brushed her mouth tantalisingly along his sexy lips.

'*Dio*. I used to lie in bed and dream of you in my arms, wake and reach for you, and find only an empty bed.' He groaned as his hand quickly unzipped her dress and pushed it from her shoulders. He gazed with feverish eyes on the soft curve of her breasts. 'Now I have you, I still wake in the night and simply watch you, terrified of losing you.'

'I had noticed,' Kelly confessed. Stunned by the golden glare of love in his eyes, the wonder of his love washing over her like a healing balm, Kelly did some undressing of her own.

'Not the sofa. Bed,' Gianfranco muttered frantically a few minutes later as he lifted her in his arms, he carried her into the bedroom and laid her gently on the bed. Sitting on the bed, in a trice he had dispensed with their clothes and swung his long legs up. He stretched out at her side, and, supporting himself on one elbow, stared down at her naked body.

One hand almost tentatively spread out over her flat stomach. 'I can't believe we have made a baby again the first time we made love after three years.' His hand swept up over her midriff and over the firm swell of one breast.

Kelly breathed a deep, shaky breath, trembling at the force of her emotions. 'You really don't mind?'

Gianfranco groaned and captured her mouth with his in a deeply tender kiss—a kiss like no other they had shared, an avowal of love and tenderness, commitment and hope. Finally he lifted his head and looked down at her. 'I love you, Kelly, and I want you to have my baby.' His dark eyes held hers, and surprisingly she discerned a certain vulnerability in their depths.

'But...?' she prompted, her body burning for him, and her heart suddenly fearful again as he hesitated, holding a terrific control over his emotions.

'Watching Anna and her groom and Annalou at the wedding today, listening to our daughter talking tonight, I realised I cheated you out of so many things. Kelly, will you marry me again—in church, with all our friends and neighbours and my mother in attendance?' He touched his lips to the elegant curve of her throat. 'I want there to be no doubt in your mind you are my wife and I love you.'

Meeting his eyes, Kelly parted her lips in a slow, sensual smile. 'Good idea,' she murmured throatily. Her small hands stroking up over his broad chest with tactile pleasure before curving around his neck, she pulled his head down and pressed a light kiss on his bruised nose. 'Sorry about the punch,' she apologised softly. 'But if you think for one moment I am going to be a pregnant bride for a second time, I'll give you another!' she teased. 'Try asking me again when I am not pregnant.'

Twelve months later, Kelly stood in the grand hall of the Casa Maldini, wearing an ivory satin wedding gown studded with seed-pearls and sequins, the train extending four feet behind her, with Annalou standing watching, looking equally lovely in a fairy-tale blue dress, and Judy Bertoni as maid of honour in a similar blue gown.

Carmela was elegant in a tailored suit in a subtle shade of cinnamon but the effect was spoilt somewhat by the five-month-old baby boy she was holding in her arms, Gianni Thomaso Maldini. 'You look beautiful, Kelly,' Carmela said, 'but let's go—we are forty minutes late.'

Gianfranco paced up and down the path to the church; his easy smile when he'd first arrived had long since turned to a frown. Father Rosso was waiting to begin the service. Where the hell was Kelly?

Then he saw the limousine draw up, and a relieved smile split his handsome face. Judy and Annalou skipped out, followed by his mother and son. Then his dark eyes widened with incredulity at the woman who followed.

Kelly, a vision in yards of bejewelled satin, with her silver-blonde hair swept up in a coronet of curls held in place by a diamond tiara, took his breath away. He drew in a ragged breath, his eyes suddenly darkening with deep emotion as they met hers, and she smiled, a dazzling smile only for him that lit her sapphire eyes and put the diamonds she was wearing to shame.

His hand, holding the posy of roses, trembled as he stepped forward to present them to his bride, a traditional Italian custom. 'For you.' He pushed the posy at her.

Kelly could not help smiling. He looked incredibly handsome in a pearl-grey tailcoat and a white wing-collar shirt, with a cream and gold cravat and matching waistcoat. Tall and elegant, every inch the aristocrat. But it was the expression in his eyes that thrilled Kelly to the bone: deeply possessive and blazing with the light of love.

'You look out of this world, incredibly beautiful, and I love you with a passion, a devotion, that will live through this world and the next,' Gianfranco said in a voice not quite steady as he led her into the church.

Her eyes misting with moisture, she squeezed his hand, her heart overflowing with love. 'Thank you,' Kelly said, and in that one word she was thanking him for everything: his love, their children, their life together.

It was the wedding of the year. Family and friends, dignitaries from all over Italy, business colleagues—no one was excluded. After the service the reception was held out of doors in the grounds of Casa Maldini.

'We have to leave soon...' Gianfranco's arm was wrapped firmly around his wife's waist, where it had been all afternoon. He glanced down at Kelly, his dark eyes glinting with raw desire. 'If we want to make the flight.'

Gianfranco adored Annalou, and had been at the birth of his son Gianni, and the experience had filled him with awe and humility. But, much as he loved his family, after two weddings they were finally going to get to go on honeymoon. Alone. He could not wait to get Kelly on her own for three whole weeks.

'OK.' Kelly beamed up at him. It had to be the best wedding any woman in the world had ever had, she thought, glowing with happiness and pride for the man at her side who had done all this for her.

'We don't want to be late. You were late at the church,' Gianfranco reminded her, just as the rather loud voice of a slightly inebriated Father Rosso, who was standing behind them, boomed out.

'Two children and five years late, but they got there in the end. *Dio grazie.*'

CALL THE ONES YOU LOVE OVER THE HOLIDAYS!

Save $25 off future book purchases when you buy any four Harlequin® or Silhouette® books in October, November and December 2001,

PLUS

receive a phone card good for 15 minutes of long-distance calls to anyone you want in North America!

WHAT AN INCREDIBLE DEAL!

Just fill out this form and attach 4 proofs of purchase (cash register receipts) from October, November and December 2001 books, and Harlequin Books will send you a coupon booklet worth a total savings of $25 off future purchases of Harlequin® and Silhouette® books, AND a 15-minute phone card to call the ones you love, anywhere in North America.

Please send this form, along with your cash register receipts as proofs of purchase, to:
In the USA: Harlequin Books, P.O. Box 9057, Buffalo, NY 14269-9057
In Canada: Harlequin Books, P.O. Box 622, Fort Erie, Ontario L2A 5X3
Cash register receipts must be dated no later than December 31, 2001.
Limit of 1 coupon booklet and phone card per household.
Please allow 4-6 weeks for delivery.

I accept your offer! Enclosed are 4 proofs of purchase.
Please send me my coupon booklet
and a 15-minute phone card:

Name: _____

Address: _____ City: _____

State/Prov.: _____ Zip/Postal Code: _____

Account Number (if available): _____

---

097 KJB DAGL
PHQ4013

If you enjoyed what you just read,
then we've got an offer you can't resist!

Take 2 bestselling love stories FREE!

Plus get a FREE surprise gift!

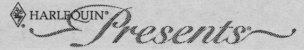

HARLEQUIN *Presents*

The world's bestselling romance series.
Seduction and passion guaranteed!

**Pick up a Harlequin Presents® novel and you will
enter a world of spine-tingling passion and
provocative, tantalizing romance!**

Join us in 2002 for an exciting selection of titles
from all your favorite authors:

Red Hot Revenge
COLE CAMERON'S REVENGE #2223, January
by Sandra Marton

Secret Passions
A truly thrilling new duet
THE SECRET VENGEANCE #2236, March
THE SECRET LOVE CHILD #2242, April
by Miranda Lee

A Mediterranean Marriage
THE BELLINI BRIDE #2224, January
by Michelle Reid
and
THE ITALIAN'S WIFE #2235, March
by Lynne Graham

An upbeat, contemporary story
THE CITY-GIRL BRIDE #2229, February
by Penny Jordan

An involving and dramatic read
A RICH MAN'S TOUCH #2230, February
by Anne Mather

On sale in the New Year
Available wherever Harlequin Books are sold.

HARLEQUIN®
Makes any time special ®

WITH HARLEQUIN AND SILHOUETTE

There's a romance to fit your every mood.

Passion

Harlequin Temptation

Harlequin Presents

Silhouette Desire

Pure Romance

Harlequin Romance

Silhouette Romance

Home & Family

Harlequin
American Romance

Silhouette
Special Edition

A Longer Story With More

Harlequin
Superromance

Suspense & Adventure

Harlequin Intrigue

Silhouette Intimate
Moments

Humor

Harlequin Duets

Historical

Harlequin Historicals

Special Releases

Other great
romances
to explore